ECHO OF

FEAR

The Chris Echo Files

TARA MEYERS

Forest Grove Books

ISBN-13: 978-1544057729

ISBN-10: 1544057725

ECHO OF FEAR

AUTHOR'S NOTE

Thank you for purchasing Echo of Fear! I hope that you find it as much fun to read, as I had writing it. If you enjoy the story, you might also want to look into my other novels, written under my pen name of Tara Ellis. You can find my author profile on Amazon. Be sure to watch for the next book in The Chris Echo Files, and if you haven't already read the free, short story, A Distant Echo, you might want to go download the ebook right now!

One

Chris
Saturday, 2:00 PM

Chris Echo lifted her face to the sun, allowing the warm, tropical breeze to engulf her. She hoped it was a cleansing breeze, because that's why she was there. Standing in the bow of the boat, she looked out at the vast expanse of water around her and fought back a wave of fear. She was used to being in control, and this was way out of her comfort zone.

This is a vacation, she chided herself. *I'm supposed to relax. That's the whole point, right?*

But no matter how many times Chris told herself that this was just a vacation, she knew the truth was much more complicated. She couldn't help but feel that she was running away from the mess she had created back home, and to where she was running, she didn't know. Was she looking for answers, for escape, or for a firmer definition of the person she'd become?

Birds eagerly circled the slow moving boat, fighting

over the handouts. A man, who appeared to be in his late fifties, stood several feet away from Chris. He was the one responsible for the annoying screeching from the scavengers. As she watched through dark sunglasses, he tossed out yet another piece of his sandwich, smiling as the birds dove for the food. The number of gulls dwindled the further they went from shore, and she imagined they would soon be gone altogether.

The man eventually looked up to meet her gaze. His wrinkled, sunburnt face was full of pleasure, much like a child that's discovered a new game. Chris couldn't help but smile back. She knew immediately that she would like this man if they got a chance to know each other.

Looking down at the worn brochure she clutched in her hands, Chris smiled again and felt a small stirring of anticipation. She practically had the pamphlet memorized, but she still unfolded the pages to look again at what promised to be a vacation in paradise. Off the corner of northwestern South America, it was a small resort on a privately owned island in the South Pacific. It boasted a master house and five neighboring cabins, all surrounded by a wide, white beach. Meals were served in the main house, and the only thing you had to worry about, it claimed, was dressing yourself and getting too much sun.

It's exactly what I need, Chris told herself for the hundredth time. *Two weeks with absolutely nothing to do but relax.*

Watching the receding mainland, she tried to keep smiling. Her hand went automatically to her back pocket in search of her phone before she could stop herself. Her lifeline was safely packed away in her suitcase, snuggled up next to her laptop.

In the year and a half that Chris had been working for the Seattle PD as a crime scene investigator, she had taken very little time off. In fact, during the six years prior to her promotion from detective to CSI, Chris could count on one hand the number of times she'd ever been out of town for more than a day or two that wasn't business-related. And she couldn't remember a time that she wasn't available by phone. It was impossible to keep her out of the office if there was an active investigation underway.

Unless you count my mandatory suspension, she thought, her grin fading.

Three months before Mick, her supervisor, 'advised' her to take her vacation days, Chris Echo had killed a man.

He was a suspect in a possible serial murder case. Chris, as usual, had pushed harder than she should have and made herself a target. The bloody scene in her secluded cabin took the state forensics team days to process while she was on mandatory paid leave. It was another two weeks before the prosecutor determined he wasn't going to bring her up on charges for a wrongful death.

Chris could have cared less about her own legal issues. While all of that was going on, her partner, Andrew, had been fighting for his life after taking a bullet for her. No matter how many times he tried to convince her it wasn't her fault, she knew it was. Her reckless desire to solve the case on her own led to the confrontation he unknowingly walked into.

Closing her eyes against the memory, Chris ignored the increasing tightness in her chest and focused on slowing her breathing. The anxiety attacks were getting worse. She'd been through counseling, as a teen, after a traumatic incident, so she had good coping skills … but everyone has their limits.

Andrew pulled through and was expected to make a full recovery. Martin Eastabrooke remained very much dead because of a gunshot wound to the head: an act by Chris that was determined to be self-defense. But she knew the truth. A truth she'd decided in a split-second of time that she could live with.

But it wasn't quite that easy.

One week after the state cleared her, Mick called Chris into the office and unceremoniously returned her badge and gun. She promptly threw herself back into her active caseload and tried not to look back.

Two months later, with winter approaching and yet another year without putting in for vacation time, Mick put his foot down. While the threat was veiled, he made it clear that she needed to either find a way to get herself right in the head, or else he'd force her into counseling. According to him, he wasn't the only team member to notice her long work hours, the bags under her eyes, and her declining physical fitness.

I need this, Chris reminded herself, pushing away from the railing with resolution. *I need to concentrate on myself for a while and make sure that I'm still in there somewhere, that I am more than just my career.*

At thirty-two, she'd never had a serious relationship that had even come close to marriage, and she only rarely dated. Not that she wasn't attractive; she just didn't make herself available.

Chris undid her long, bronze hair from its holder, letting the wind swirl it around her face and shoulders. Her heart-shaped face and full lips at first gave the impression of a young, naïve girl. However, the bold, direct gaze of her green eyes revealed her inner strength. At 5'10" with an athletic build, Chris learned early on to use her size to her advantage. In her profession, she often had to deal with men who believed that women couldn't handle the job. Chris very rarely backed down from a confrontation and was known for her temper and quick tongue.

Playing the vacationer was not an easy role for her. But she decided that if she was doing this, she was going to do it right. Like everything else she tackled, Chris did so with vigor. She'd dug out her camera, purchased the proper attire, and had gone to the tanning booth a few times to avoid burning.

As a result of the shooting incident, Chris had fallen into a slump. She refused to call it depression, but the results were the same. Her visits to the gym declined, the amount of wine she drank increased, and she avoided her normal stress relievers like running on the trails in the woods near her cabin.

Deciding she could stand to trim off a few pounds before donning her new bikini, Chris signed up for an additional defense class. She also returned to her normal workout routine and put in an extra hour twice a week in a Zumba class, the new rage at her gym. She kept the hot pink bikini hung on her closet door as an incentive. It was now stashed away in her suitcase, right next to her service revolver and department ID.

While packing the day before, Chris found that she just couldn't leave the items behind. She might be taking the trip her supervisor had practically ordered, but she would always be an officer no matter where she went. The additional paperwork at the airport had almost caused her to miss her plane. It wouldn't have even been possible if not for her previous travel for official business.

Shaking her head to clear it of the work-related thoughts, Chris tried to shift into tourist mode. There were other people on the boat, so she turned around to observe the group she was sharing this adventure with.

On the other side of the deck, a young teenager around fifteen lay sprawled across a lounge chair, an earpiece trailing back to some invisible digital device hidden somewhere on him. Apparently, there was still some reception because the teen was feverishly texting someone. Even while Chris scrutinized his blind absorption, she longed for the comfort of her own phone and had to, once again, stop herself from reaching for it.

Next to the teen stood a man that Chris could only assume was his father. He seemed rather lost. She prided herself in being able to read a person; after all, it was part of her job. He looked to be a middle-aged, white male with somewhat of a gut and was a little pale. Probably had a job that kept him behind a desk most of the time. He fit the typical serial killer profile.

Damn it! What am I doing? Chris chastised herself. *Can't I leave it alone for one day?*

Determined to have a real vacation, she crossed the small deck and walked up to the 'serial killer' to introduce herself. "Hi!" She said cheerfully, "My name is Chris Echo. Are you headed for Carter's resort, too?"

Taking her hand in a much firmer grasp than Chris expected, the man pumped her arm enthusiastically.

"Ken Swanson. This is my son, David." He placed his hand on the boys shoulder.

David removed his sunglasses and looked at his father's hand as if it were a snake. Peering up at Chris, however, his demeanor quickly changed. He smiled broadly, revealing perfectly white teeth against his darker complexion. Chris guessed that his mom must be African American. Pulling the earphones out, he snapped his phone shut.

"Yes," Ken continued, not seeming to notice the slight from his son. "We're staying at the resort for a week. It's supposed to be a beautiful place. I could certainly use the sun!" he added good-naturedly, patting his pale face. "I spend all my time indoors, programming computers. We're from Denver, Colorado."

"I live in Seattle, Washington." Chris offered, but intentionally failed to explain her profession. She knew from experience that people viewed her differently when they found out she worked for the police. She didn't want that on this trip.

Chris noticed that David was still grinning at her with obvious admiration.

"Hey, how you doin'?" He asked flippantly, trying his best to sound cool.

Before the situation became too awkward, the gentleman who had been feeding the birds walked up. Brushing the crumbs from his pants, he then shook hands with everyone, smiling broadly.

"Hope you don't mind my interrupting," he said brightly. "But I figure if we're going to all be spending some time together on that little island, we ought to get to know one another. My name's George Miley," he continued, making a point to include David in his greeting. "This trip is sort of an overdue retirement celebration for me. I flew all the way down from Canada. A close friend of mine insists that this place is heaven on earth." Chris and the others repeated their introductions with George.

He's just like your stereotypical sea captain, Chris thought, noting his salt and pepper hair, stubbly chin, and broad chest.

As he laughed heartily at something Ken said, Chris's earlier suspicions were confirmed. She liked this man immensely. His passion for life was apparent, and she found it refreshing just to be in his presence.

Perhaps I will enjoy this trip as much as I hoped, Chris considered.

With good company and a sun-soaked beach, what could go wrong?

Two

Chris
Saturday, 4:30 P.M.

Chris paused long enough on the dock to look back at the boat that was heading away from the island.

This is your last chance, she told herself. *If you yell now, they can probably still hear you.*

She actually considered doing it. But then Chris heard the waves crashing on the beach and the birds calling from the jungle behind her and realized that this was where she wanted to be. Turning back around, she adjusted the large duffel bag across her shoulder, and hefted the suitcase that she practically wrestled away from George.

A well-kept trail led back into the trees, and Chris could just make out the top of the main house, complete with a widows walk.

A slight, native-looking woman was waiting on the dock for them when the boat arrived. Now the small group followed the guide through the growth in a rough, single line. She introduced herself as Karen Valdez, the maid and program coordinator for the resort. With impressively precise English, she revealed that her husband was the groundskeeper and that they lived in one of the cabins.

"You're just going to love your stay here," she said sincerely while spreading her arms wide. "My husband and I are native to this region. This island has always been a favorite spot of ours, and we were thrilled when the Carter's opened the resort. The previous two owners were very private, and it was difficult to get permission to visit. If you ever need anything like towels or drinks and such for the cabins, please let me know. I can also show you around the island. There are some amazing spots for hiking!"

A man and woman greeted them from a large wraparound porch as soon as the house came into view.

"Welcome to Carter's Resort!" the friendly woman called out. "I'm Dorothy Carter, and this is my husband, Max," she explained as they all climbed up the front steps.

The older couple was as spirited as someone half their age and welcomed each new guest with obvious pleasure.

"If you'd like to set your things here, just inside the door, we'll give you a quick tour of the house," Dorothy continued. "Then we'll show you where your cabins are. Dinner will be served within the hour, so you should have time to get your things put away!" With that, she spun on her heels and walked away quickly through the grand foyer.

Chris paused in the entrance, startled to discover a completely unexpected décor. The brochure focused on the beaches and cabins and only had a couple photos of the main house, one taken from the outside. The only interior image showed the dining room, and Chris had thought nothing of the rich woodwork it featured. However, that theme was carried throughout the entire structure. She stood gazing at massive, rough-hewn wood beams that supported a two-story great room. A check-in desk was across from them with a sitting area off to the left. The accompanying furnishings and over-all atmosphere lent to an experience you'd expect at a lodge in Alaska, not a tropical island. Chris loved it.

Their host dashed through an arched entryway to the right. "This is the recreation room," Dorothy called out, encouraging everyone to gather in behind her.

It was an even larger room with the same open beam design. A collection of couches and easy chairs were at the opposite end, arranged in front of a massive, natural-stone fireplace. In the center stood a grand pool table with elaborately carved wooden legs, and a dartboard and gaming table were conveniently placed in the remaining space.

The walls were paneled in a rich cherry-wood, bathed in sunlight pouring in through large, two-story windows lining the front of the house. A couple of Navaho throw rugs, scattered on the wood floor, completed the warm atmosphere of the room.

It was a stark contrast to the island scene outside, but

it somehow felt right. Chris could see herself spending time relaxing there in the evening hours. Her conviction that this trip was good for her continued to grow.

"My wife wanted a warm, tropical climate retirement while I longed to discover my inner cowboy," Max said good-naturedly. "I compromised."

Ignoring her husband, Dorothy walked over to the only other door in the room. "Feel free to use this game room or the den anytime. The den is just through here," she explained, taking a step into a much smaller space. "The front door of the main house is never locked. There's no need!"

"Now, I expect to get a chance at beating you in a game of pool later this evening," George said to Chris, smiling.

"Oh, you'll get a game," Chris replied. "But don't count on winning!"

George erupted into laughter once again, patting her shoulder as if she was an old friend. To her surprise, Chris found that she didn't mind. He reminded her of her father, she suddenly realized. Not at all in personality, but in looks. Her own father was much more reserved. She couldn't remember a time when she had felt as comfortable with him as she did with George.

Her mother was killed in a car wreck when she was just a young girl. Unable to handle the responsibility of raising a small child on his own, her father sent her to live with his parents. He provided for everything she needed and used to visit her frequently, but then it slowly turned into only on the holidays. After the … incident when she was sixteen, she rarely saw him anymore.

Chris found herself wondering why that was. He didn't live that far away. Who was to blame for it? *Perhaps we both are,* she speculated, watching David as he attempted to make his phone work. Ken stood next to him, trying to offer suggestions. *Here's a man so eager to have a relationship with his child. What makes one parent care and another seem to not give it a second though?* Shaking her head to snap out of her musings, Chris vowed to call her father when she got home. With the recent shooting, she'd almost called him twice. He was a successful surgeon and still actively working, but he'd gone into semi-retirement five years ago. Had she spoken to him since then? At least she could try and the rest would be up to him.

Dorothy walked further into the den with her husband close behind. Other than smiling at everything his wife said, he didn't add much and seemed content with having her lead the tour.

The quaint room was the model of your typical den, complete with wall-to-wall bookcases and two overstuffed chairs in opposite corners. The only entrance was the one through the recreation room. After they all filed in, Dorothy pointed to a large wooden desk. "This computer is the only other means of communicating with the mainland besides the radio," she explained. "Any of you are welcome to use it, but please ask Max or myself for assistance. It's an older system and is prone to interruptions in service." At this announcement, David looked up sharply from his non-working phone.

"Do you mean that there's no cell phone service or

Wifi here?" David practically yelled with rising panic in his voice. He stared accusingly at his father as if he was leading a conspiracy against him.

"Nope. No cell service or internet except for in here," Ken explained. "Sorry if you were unaware, but it explains all of that in the brochure. It's one of the reasons some people choose to come here."

David looked incredulously at his dad, his suspicions confirmed. Obviously, he hadn't shared the news with his son.

Chris thought once again of the electronic devices in her suitcase. As much as she missed them, she was glad the temptation was removed. Although, she knew for a fact they would be out and turned on the second she was back in range. They'd be used non-stop during her two-day trip back home.

Grinning at the on-going drama between father and son, Chris turned her attention back to their hosts. She was curious to see the rest of the house. It had a unique floor plan.

Dorothy was true to her word, and the rest of the tour went very quickly. To the left of the main entrance and opposite the recreation room was the pictured dining hall. It had a matching fireplace on the far wall and the same large windows on the front, facing west. Down the middle ran a huge oak table capable of seating around twenty-five people. They peeked through two swinging doors on the back wall that opened into a gourmet kitchen a professional chef would be proud to work in.

Chris had begun to smell something amazing while

they were in the rec room, and they appeared to have found the source of the wonderful aromas. Breathing deeply, she looked with interest at the food on the stoves. She didn't realize how hungry she was.

The cook was introduced as Esmeralda, who nodded her hellos as she went busily about making dinner for everyone. "Esmeralda is a dear friend of ours and lives here in the main house," Dorothy explained. "She's an Islander, like Karen and Rico, but much more traditional. Her cooking is wonderful, and please feel free to ask for anything, anytime."

Apparently, David was even hungrier than Chris was and not so upset by his forced isolation that it affected his appetite. He immediately took advantage of the offer and grabbed a couple of rolls off a nearby counter. Appalled, Ken snatched them from his son, apologizing to their host.

"She said we could have whatever we wanted," David whined, crossing his arms in an expression very close to a pout more appropriate for a child half his age.

"You ask," Ken admonished. "You don't just take it!"

"Oh, that's okay," Dorothy said lightly. "Go ahead and let him have them. I should have asked you all if you needed anything when you first arrived. How about something to drink?" Taking her up on the offer, they all selected a beverage and then went on to see the rest of the house.

What Chris had assumed to be a door to a closet behind the reception counter turned out to be another small room. It contained the radio that they used as their main source of communication with the mainland. The room also served as an office where they stored all the paperwork associated with running the resort. Its only window peered out into the thick jungle that was held at bay not far from the house. It was wide open, and the smells and sounds that drifted in were even more enticing than those in the kitchen.

At the back of the house was a large sunroom with wicker furniture. It had a beautiful view of a tropical garden, complete with a fish pond. Just before the entrance to the sunroom was a steep stairway, which Dorothy told them led to the upstairs bedrooms.

"Where's the TV?" David asked when they had obviously seen all of the downstairs and were assembled once again by the double front doors. "I didn't see one."

"That's because there isn't one," Max replied. "Here on the island, we have nature and our imaginations, plus the company of friends, to keep us entertained." At the look of horror on the young man's face, Max laughed loudly. "Of course, if you decide your imagination isn't enough, there is a flat-screen in your cabin and a selection of DVD's in the den."

David sighed with obvious relief; but irritated at being the brunt of the joke, he stomped off to the back door and out into the gardens.

During the rest of the ride to the island earlier that day, Chris had learned that David's father, Ken, recently went through an unpleasant divorce. It was apparent to Chris that this trip was an attempt, on Ken's part, to try to patch the rift that had developed between him and his fifteen-year-old son. *Good luck,* Chris thought, watching the teen adjust his earpieces as he disappeared into the foliage.

Three

Chris
Saturday, 5:30 P.M.

Karen re-appeared to help lead them all to their respective cabins and explained that they fanned out on either side of the main house with plenty of space and privacy between them.

Dorothy took Ken, David, and George along a rock lined path to the north of the house while Chris walked with Karen in the opposite direction. The air was sweet with the tropical flowers that grew wild in the undergrowth around them. Karen was full of small talk as they strode along the trail, and she pointed out other less-worn paths that branched off from the main one as they went.

"Most of the trails are well kept," she explained. "But I would recommend you stay on them. The East side of the island gets rather steep, and it would be easy to get turned around in the heavy vegetation. We once had a guest lost for over half a day. The island isn't that big, just under three miles long and half that at its widest spot, but it's enough to keep you guessing for a while! If you would like, in the morning we can go for a hike."

Chris thought it was a great idea, and they agreed to set out after breakfast. The jungle abruptly ended and the two women were greeted with a white, pristine beach.

Chris's cabin was only a couple hundred feet from the main house, but it may as well have been on an island all its own. The view was breathtaking. Chris stood silently for several minutes, soaking it in. Karen was apparently used to this response. She stood quietly next to her, waiting. "It's beautiful," Chris finally said.

"Yes," Karen agreed. "No matter how many times I stand on this beach, it is as if I'm seeing it for the first time. This is a very special place."

The cabin turned out to be small but very comfortable. Where the house was all about rich wood and cowboys, the cottage met every tropical getaway expectation from the paint color to throw pillows. Although the floorboards creaked as they walked across the front room, it appeared sound. Chris placed her bags on the bed in the bedroom and went back and sat on a comfy, overstuffed couch. It took up a good portion of the rest of the cabin. The promised flat screen sat against the opposite wall, and there was a small refrigerator for drinks next to a tiki counter. Otherwise, the room was meant solely for admiring the scene out the large front window.

"There is a young newlywed couple in the next cabin about a hundred feet south of here. Very nice people,"

Karen explained. "They'll be leaving us on Friday when the next boat arrives." Pulling her sunglasses out of her thick, black hair, Karen waved them toward where the main house was before putting them on. "My cabin is one of the other three larger ones to the north. I'm sure you already know from the literature you received that there are only five cabins. Not too much competition for a good spot on the beach! Enjoy your stay, Chris. I'll see you in about half an hour at dinner, okay? You can meet my husband."

"I'm looking forward to it, Karen," Chris assured her as she followed the other woman outside. "Oh! I almost forgot. I was wondering if you know what the weather forecast is? I'm hoping to get lots of time in the sun during the next two weeks."

"You're in luck," Karen said. "Nothing *but* sun. There's a storm brewing out in the ocean southwest of here; but this time of year, they almost never blow inland." With that, she waved goodbye and headed back out.

Alone for the first time since her trip started, Chris walked slowly outside, kicking her sandals off as she went. As soon as her feet sank into the warm sand, she knew she had indeed found heaven.

I think maybe I should have done this a long time ago, she thought, watching the waves crash on the beach.

Closing her eyes, Chris let the calm of the island wash over her, erasing the last remnants of tension. She eventually walked towards the ocean and sat down just out of reach of the water. There were some gathering clouds on the far horizon in an otherwise clear, blue sky.

Chris fingered a piece of seaweed and marveled at how she had come to be on this beach. The irony was if it'd been left up to her, she would probably be behind her desk working through another weekend. Chris was so absorbed in her work these past years, that she' been ignoring her family and even more importantly, her own needs. Burning out by the time you were her age wasn't uncommon in her line of work, and Chris's almost obsessive desire to be the best didn't help.

After two weeks here, I just might decide to retire early and help Esmeralda out in the kitchen, she thought, a rare giggle escaping.

Voices filtering through the undergrowth brought her out of her revere. Turning, Chris could just make out movement on the trail behind her cabin. Assuming they were her neighbors, she glanced at her watch and was amazed at how long she'd been staring out at the ocean. She would be late for dinner if she didn't hurry.

***

The dining hall was filled with pleasant conversation as Esmeralda cleared the dinner plates. The young newlyweds, Desmond and Cathy Laurent, proved be as charming as Karen said they'd be. Obviously in love, they spent most of the evening gazing at each other, and Chris couldn't help but feel a little envious. Desmond had the dark, sharp features of a European, but Chris couldn't tell if he was French or Italian. Either way, he lacked an accent and his demeanor screamed American military.

Cathy quickly confirmed this. "I'm finishing school while Desmond serves his four years in the Marines," she explained, toying with the new ring on her finger. With her blonde hair pulled back in a ponytail, the petite woman looked barely old enough to be married.

With Karen on one side and George on the other, it was a challenge for Chris to get her food eaten. When not working to keep up on the constant chatter around her, she studied the other people gathered at the table. Karen's husband, Rico, was a large, quiet man, in direct contrast to his wife. Chris noticed that David ignored his father's attempts to talk with him, but at least he lost the earphones. With his shoulder length hair tucked behind his ears, he looked quite normal. *Maybe there's hope for him yet,* Chris thought, suppressing a smile.

As dessert was being dished out, Max grabbed a cookie before excusing himself to go see to some things. Chris watched him leave and noticed his brief, nervous glance at Dorothy. *What was that about?*

"So, are you all settled into your cabin?" George inquired after sipping at his wine, unaware of the tension Chris detected. "Mine is just wonderful. My wife would have loved it." When Chris didn't answer right away, he looked at her with pain evident in his blue eyes. "Celeste passed away five years ago. That's why I've waited to take this trip. I felt guilty about doing it before." He twirled the wineglass slowly as he spoke, the amber liquid almost spilling. "I guess there just comes a time when you realize what your loved one would have wanted is for you to get off your sorry ass and do something!"

Sensing he didn't want, or need any sympathy, Chris just nodded and covered his callused hand with her own.

When he met her gaze again, the sorrow was gone and the sparkle back. "Come then!" He almost shouted, slapping the table. "Let's go play that game."

"Just let me finish this wonderful piece of chocolate cake and then I'm all yours," Chris said, taking a big bite.

George admired her hearty appetite before leaning across the table to answer a question Ken was asking. When Max returned minutes later, he quickly went to his wife and spoke in hushed tones. The atmosphere in the room changed quickly, and Chris felt a familiar tingling sensation at the base of her neck. Something was most definitely up.

"Um, I need to have your attention for a moment," Max said to the group of vacationers. "It would seem a tropical storm out at sea has taken an unexpected turn inland. It's supposed to make landfall sometime tomorrow, and we are in its path." He raised his hands to quiet all the voices that suddenly erupted with questions. "By the time it reaches us, it may very well be at a hurricane level," he continued when everyone calmed down. "Now, it isn't expected to last more than two days, tops. The worst of it will probably pass within twenty-four hours of its beginning. There'll still be time in the morning to call a launch over to take you back to the mainland. But to tell you the truth, we're probably better prepared than the hotels you would find with vacancies. The cabins all have shutters and the island is already self-contained with generators and such. Of course, you would all stay here in the main house for one night, just to be safe. It's not a very dangerous storm if you're on land, just enough to keep us all indoors and battened down for a bit. These structures have been through much worse." Max looked at everyone in the room and shrugged. "It's up to you whether you stay or go. Just let me know by morning so I can radio the boat."

They all started talking at once again, but it wasn't long before there was an agreement that everyone would stay. It didn't make sense to leave the island when they would be just as good, or even better off, where they were.

Slouching down in her chair, Chris pulled her heavy hair away from her face and lifted it off the back of her neck. She wasn't sure if the humidity actually took a sudden jump, or if it was nerves causing the sweat to break out. Closing her eyes, she concentrated on forcing back the caged-up feeling already pressing in.

Typical, she thought, letting a sigh escape. *I should have known this trip wasn't going to be normal.*

Four

Kyle
Sunday, 12:00 P.M.

Kyle Stone squinted against the hot afternoon sun. He was getting a headache.

Leaning casually over the railing of the mid-sized boat, he closed his eyes and worked on calming his nerves. You would never know by his demeanor that there was a war of conflicting emotions raging inside. While his tanned face bore some telltale wrinkles around the eyes, he still looked young for his thirty-five years. The older he got, the harder he had to work to keep his physique, but his reputation as a solid fighter was well known among the Guerrillas.

Behind him, two men were yelling back and forth at each other in Spanish as they made final preparations for their overnight voyage. They were both locals from Guatemala, and hired guns. Kyle was a couple of rungs up the ladder in the radical organization, even though he was the only gringo in the inner circle.

He was also the only CIA agent. Well, as far as he knew. Pushing away from the rail, he stopped himself from wiping his palms on his jeans. Instead, he pushed his dark, sweaty hair out of his eyes and scratched at his customary three-day growth of beard. Studying the surrounding moored boats, he looked for anything out of the norm. His steel-grey eyes were intelligent and mysterious, so he'd been told. He supposed that was due to his ability to wear a poker face on demand; and for the past couple of years, that was most of the time.

"Since when did I start paying you to stand around and daydream?"

Turning, Kyle caught a large duffle bag as it slammed into his chest. Grinning crookedly at his leader, he held on tight to the valuable cargo. "What you call daydreaming, Jose, I call careful observation. Speaking of slackers, where the hell is Carlos?"

The fifth, and last, man going on the current exploit was late. Considering the importance of the at-sea exchange, he was surprised Jose wasn't already cursing him.

Shrugging, Jose dropped a second bag on the deck. "He had a couple of errands to run. He'll be here. Take both of these down below," he directed, unwilling to give any further explanation.

The older extremist tended to keep the details of his operations guarded, but part of Kyle's job was to make sure things ran smoothly. He didn't like being out of the loop, especially where Carlos was involved. The two of them had been vying for the honorary position of Jose's right-hand-man for months.

His unease growing, Kyle pointed to the distant horizon of the Pacific Ocean. Knowing better than to push the issue, he changed the subject. "I don't like those clouds."

Jose raised a hand to shield his eyes and studied the buildup of an impressive storm front. It was so far away, however, that it didn't appear to pose a threat. "I thought you said the forecast was for it to stay well to the south of us."

Scratching again at his jawline, Kyle chose his words carefully. Ideally, if he could get him to move up the drop to earlier in the day, it would make it much easier for his associates to make the bust. Even if he got the GPS coordinates transmitted once he knew them, the final assault would be much more effective if done in daylight.

"Forecasts are often wrong," he said stoically. "I was listening to some of the locals. Take a look," he directed, gesturing to the boat next to them. "Apparently, something the weatherman is missing has got them riled."

Jose watched for a few minutes as the bare-chested fishermen worked to batten down their vessel. While their motions were smooth and well-practiced, there was an undeniable air of urgency. Turning, he studied the other boats that were also in their slips and saw several similar undertakings.

Waving a dismissive hand, Jose chortled. "Superstition. A dolphin probably looked at one of them the wrong way. I'll stick to the official meteorological report. Which *you* gave me," he added.

Nodding, Kyle knew better than to not agree. "Right. Just doing a thorough job. None of us are very experienced boatmen. I figured it might not hurt to move the schedule up. If we get out there and have our asses handed to us, you can't blame the dolphins."

Laughing at the poor attempt at a joke, Jose threw the second bag at him. "No changes," he stated. "And I'm counting on you to make sure of that."

Discouraged but not surprised, Kyle headed for the cabin and the lower rooms of the boat. After stowing the payload, he paused to listen to Felipe and Fredrick argue over the condition of the engine. Shaking his head after a few minutes, he went into the small space that housed his bunk. Kneeling down, he rummaged in his personal belongings. Pulling a disposable phone from a hidden compartment, he sent the last message he'd be able to get out before losing a signal. After that, he'd have to use the SAT phone he had hidden in a false wall behind the bed. Both devices were a huge risk that could easily cost him his life, but everything boiled down to the next few hours. Without the communication, interception of the exchange would be impossible, and that was the whole reason he was there. And at this point, he was willing to do anything to end it.

It's a go. Still night exchange. Will send location. Be ready.

Palming the small phone, Kyle made his way back onto the deck. It only took a moment for him to see Jose was back on land, talking to Carlos in the dirt parking lot of the small marina. Making his way to the bow of the boat, he waited until the phone vibrated in his hand with the confirmation text before letting it slip into the water. Once again, he was on his own. The story of his life.

Five

Chris
Sunday, 12:30 P.M.

Chris ducked to avoid a leafy branch snapping back at her and laughed at Karen's shocked expression when she turned around at the sound.

"Sorry!" Karen called out. "It slipped."

"No harm done," Chris assured her guide.

They'd been trekking through the island jungle since eight that morning. It was an experience she was likely to never forget. Living in Washington State, Chris had explored miles of trials in the various state and national parks, but the raw beauty of the island was unlike anything she'd ever seen. From the sweeping vistas to plunging ravines, the overlying greenery lent it a magical atmosphere. She now understood why Karen and Rico were so eager to live and work there.

Studying the back of her new friend, Chris tried to guess her age. She used to be good at this, but the older she got ... the more difficult it was to discern. *Twenty-two?*

Maybe. No older than twenty-three, though. Rico could be closer to twenty-five.

"So, Karen," Chris said hesitantly. "Do you mind if I ask your age?"

"I'm twenty-six," the young woman answered with ease. "Rico will be thirty later this year."

Chris shook her head in disbelief. As a profiler by profession, she should be more accurate. Granted, they were native to a local region she'd never seen or been exposed to before, but Chris saw that as an excuse. "Any kids in your future?" she asked, interrupting her self-criticism.

Pausing on the barely distinguishable trail, Karen turned and covered her mouth to stifle a shy giggle. "Our first child will be born in five months," she revealed while dropping both of her hands to gently pat her still-flat stomach.

"Oh!" Chris gasped. "Congratulations, Karen! Are you and Rico going to stay here on the island?"

Nodding, Karen turned and started back out at a brisker pace. "Dorothy and Max are dear friends. They've offered to have us remain in our two-bedroom cabin for as long as we like, rent-free, even though I will be limited in my work once the baby is born. Rico will continue his employment, of course, and we plan to raise our family here."

Chris felt a brief pang of … what? Regret? Nostalgia? Stopping to stare solemnly at an incredibly shaped blue flower, she tried to be honest with herself. At thirty-two, most women were married and had children, or at least were seriously thinking about doing one or both things. Not her. She'd never been engaged, let-alone considered having a child. Not that Chris believed you had to have either to be happy, but when she was younger, it was what she viewed as 'normal'. A lot had happened since then.

"I'm sorry, Chris, but we need to keep moving," Karen gently urged. "I should have already been back by now to help with lunch."

Hesitating, Chris looked around at the small clearing they were standing in. She recognized it and felt somewhat confident she could find her way back, but her desire to spend the rest of the day on the beach overrode the need to explore. "We better hurry, then!" she said, breaking out in a wide smile. "I don't want anyone to complain that I'm hogging all your time!"

Giggling again, Karen broke out into a jog. As Chris followed, the trees rushed by and long grass slapped at her legs, reminding her of the trail she ran on daily near her own home. After five minutes though, she was tempted to caution Karen not to push herself so hard in her 'condition', but it would be too obvious that the plea was for her own sake. The humidity on the island was far greater than what she was used to at home, and it was kicking her butt.

Thankfully, it was only a few more minutes until they stumbled out onto the beach where Chris collapsed onto the warm sand. She watched in disbelief as Karen waved happily at her before turning to run north towards the main house.

"I don't even think she's sweating!" Chris gasped. Rolling over onto her back, she spent a few minutes gazing up at the passing clouds as her heart rate headed back down into a somewhat normal range. Lulled by the sound of the waves lapping along the shore, she would have fallen asleep if it wasn't for the intense afternoon heat. Already soaked through with sweat, Chris wrinkled her nose when the faint breeze stopped. She smelled terrible.

Pushing up onto her elbows, she looked out at the sparkling blue water and smiled at the reality of where she was. Rather than take a shower, she'd go put her suit on!

Opting for an apple from a basket of provided fruit and a granola bar she'd brought along, Chris skipped lunch and spent the afternoon swimming and sunbathing. If she was going to be holed up inside for the next twenty-four hours, the food could wait.

By late afternoon, the clouds were nearly swirling overhead, blocking out the sun, and the pressure dropped rapidly. Chris was just gathering up her beach supplies after the sunlight faded when the air around her suddenly seemed to push in on her. She could feel the tension, the pent up fury about to be released, and she rushed to her cabin to get her bag.

She'd already re-packed it with the things she would need for her one night sleepover at the main house. To prove to herself that she *was* getting into the whole vacation thing, Chris left her gun and credentials in her other suitcase. Instead, she took a book and started out just as the first drops started to fall.

Walking down the darkening trail, there was an eerie calm. Not a whisper of wind or any sounds coming from the jungle. It was as if everything was holding its breath, and Chris hoped she would make it to cover before it was let back out.

She arrived at the house to find everyone else already there. Dinner was being dished out, and Karen looked relieved when she spotted her.

"Dorothy was about to send Rico to get you!" her friend scolded while taking her bag. "I'll take this upstairs to a guest room. *You* sit down. You must be starving! I didn't see you at lunch."

"How can a girl think about eating with all of that beach to sleep on?" Chris joked. Happy to follow orders, she found an empty chair next to George again and gave him a warm greeting.

"You look like you got some sun!" the older man said with approval.

Smiling in answer, Chris turned her focus to the amazing-smelling roast. Unlike the night before, a hush fell over the table as everyone dug into the food. The island seemed to have a way of breathing both life and appetite into them, Chris observed.

Before they got through the main course, the storm suddenly erupted. Max was just informing them it was upgraded as he'd predicted but wasn't supposed to pass a category two hurricane. Chris didn't know what a category two storm was like, but the shrieking wind that abruptly began lashing at the walls and torrential rains that drowned out any conversation scared the hell out of her.

Skipping dessert, Chris made a beeline for the couch next to the fireplace. Huge wooden shutters covered the large windows, so the warm glow of the fire was inviting in the shadowed room. The temperature plummeted as soon as the rain started, and although it would still be considered warm by most standards, the drastic change combined with the dampness lent a definite chill to the air.

Wrapping up in a blanket she found on the couch, Chris wished she could see outside. The wind blew the rain against the shuttered windows of the house with such force that it sounded like small rocks. George was explaining to Ken and David that a category two meant the wind would be around a hundred miles per hour, less than what Max said the structures could hold up against.

If he says so, Chris thought while eyeing the walls around her. *This place must be well over fifty years old, probably a lot more. Maybe that's a good thing, though. It proves it's tough.*

An hour later, Chris decided it was time to take her mind off the building storm. Her historical romance wasn't quite cutting it. Marking her spot in the book, she shed the blanket and went over to where Max and George were deeply engrossed in their fourth pool match of the evening. George mockingly refused to play with Chris again after losing four times in a row the night before.

"How's it going, George?" she asked sweetly, leaning over the table. "Looks like you might be able to use a few pointers."

George looked up slowly from where he was lining up a shot and gave her a mock evil eye. "This, my dear," he said, missing his mark again, "is what is called bluffing the opponent. I almost have Max here convinced I can't play, and I'm about to make a large wager, which I then surprisingly win. Now, go! Before you ruin my whole scheme!"

Laughing, Chris shook her head and turned to Max. "Uh, when you're done being taken here, I was wondering if you could show me how to use the computer. I wanted to check my email."

Grinning, Max sunk the eight ball into his called pocket. "I can show you right now!" he laughed, handing his cue stick over to a grumbling George. "I doubt the satellite relay is going to work in this weather, but we can sure give it a shot. At least this way you'll know how to do it. Anybody else want to see how it's done?" he asked, turning to the rest of his guests.

"I'd like to, although I don't know if I really want to wade through all my emails right now." Desmond said from where he and Cathy were engaged in a game of chess.

Dorothy walked in with some fresh drinks and sat down in the spot Desmond vacated. "Mind if I take over?" she asked.

"Oh, please do!" Cathy replied, smiling.

David slammed the dart he was pulling from the board back into the bulls-eye. "Count me in!" he announced, heading quickly for the den. "My friends probably think I drowned on my way here." Ken put a hand out to stop him, but David quickly shrugged it off. "You may have sworn off your precious computers for the trip," David snapped at him, "but that doesn't mean I have to be in the dark ages. I didn't even want to come here."

Ken looked stung by the biting words but quickly composed himself. "Fine, go ahead," he said to his son's back. "We can finish the game when you're done."

David shrugged in response without turning back around.

As the four of them headed for the den, an especially large gust of wind slammed into the house, making it groan against the storm. The hairs once again rose on the back of Chris's neck. Fighting off a chill, she looked slowly around the room, thinking of the darkness that was gathering outside. In all her years as a cop and now as a CSI, she'd learned to listen to her gut. More than the night was approaching, and she couldn't credit the hurricane with the growing gnawing sensation she had. Something *was* up, and it wasn't just the storm.

Six

Kyle
Sunday, 8:00 P.M.

Kyle swore vehemently under his breath as the boat was tossed relentlessly by yet another roller. They were in trouble, and everything, *everything* could be ruined.

Two years of my life, he thought desperately. *It could all be for nothing if I don't figure out a way to pull this off.*

"You bought us a damn *sponge,* Kyle!" Jose yelled over the storm. Nostrils flaring, he glared at Kyle from across an old, scarred table, its contents now scattered around the small cabin. His unkempt, dark hair hung limply to his shoulders, streaks of gray barely visible at the hairline. His brown skin glistened with sweat as he fought to control his rage. What he lacked in height was countered by his broadness. He carried himself with the aloofness of someone accustomed to power, and he didn't like surprises.

"I chose you for this job because I *trusted* you to do it right! If we aren't at the rendezvous site, the Chinese will be gone, and they won't be coming back. Comprende?" He slammed his fists on the table for emphasis then lost his balance as the boat pitched again. He fell to the floor, cursing in Spanish.

Kyle tried to keep his temper in check and seeing Jose roll around on the floor a bit helped. It wouldn't do him any good to fight with him now. He was in a precarious enough position as it was. Kyle thought about the SAT phone below deck where the seawater was quickly collecting, and his heart raced a bit more.

"I got the boat we needed to get the job done," Kyle tried to explain rationally as Jose picked himself up. "You demanded something that would transport those guns back without being suspicious. I *told* you two hours ago that the storm shifted! If you'd listened to me, we wouldn't *be* in this freaking mess!"

"You said a *tropical storm* was building. The boat is sinking!" Jose's words were emphasized as a gigantic wave crashed over the deck of the boat.

"It's been upgraded," Kyle explained, his patience running out. "I've been trying to tell you that for the past ten minutes! We're headed into a hurricane. If we don't turn the boat around *now*, those sump pumps won't be able to keep up and we *will* sink!"

"But Chang is expecting us to radio them in another hour to get the final coordinates. If we can't meet them -- "

"To hell with the Chinese!" Kyle interrupted. "They're in the same storm. They're going to have to ride this further out to sea and won't be able to make the rendezvous, either." Kyle tensed, ready for his direct challenge to cause an assault from any direction.

Jose Cortez had been the head of a sizeable band of Guerillas for over a decade. In the last five years, he graduated from simple drug trafficking to arms. What started as a nuisance quickly became a growing concern for the US officials as more illegal weapons sold by Cortez turned up in raids on U.S. soil. Cortez's supplier was a very reclusive arms dealer in China and was the main source for the automatic rifles smuggled into the U.S. He was also Kyle's ultimate target.

Kyle had worked for the CIA for almost ten years, the last two undercover with Jose and his group. He was originally sent in as a simple contact. He would coordinate covert drop points for deliveries and information exchanges. However, that changed when Kyle began meeting with Jose Cortez himself. He then spent more time building a *deeper* cover, and he thought he could handle it. But a year later, he stood in the empty house he and his ex-wife once shared and realized, too late, that he was in over his head. He'd lost sight of who he'd become, and he was still trying to figure it out.

Staring back into the crazed eyes of Jose, he didn't dare look away. Jose would see it as a sign of weakness or indecision and lose confidence. Kyle saw this happen several times before with other 'Lieutenants'. He couldn't take any chances right now. *Not when I'm so damn close to ending this charade,* he thought.

Once the final coordinates were given, he'd use the SAT phone to reach the Coast Guard. When they had the arms supplier, their boat would be seized and he could finally arrest Jose and his group. Kyle would be free.

His chest tightened as he thought about returning to the office and trying to pick up where he'd left off. He simply wasn't the same person. With his goal so close in sight, Kyle realized that while he couldn't wait to say goodbye to the drug-dealing, violent criminal he portrayed ... he feared facing what was left.

Another sharp pitch of the boat brought him back to reality, and he watched as Jose slowly turned from him and studied the raging sea that thrashed around them. The swells were approaching fifteen feet and the sky was an angry black mess. Torrential rain was almost sideways in the wind, like a waterfall rushing horizontally. The intensity of it was building. They were running out of time.

"Okay!" Jose barked. "Turn it around, Carlos!" he yelled to the other man in the cabin. Carlos, his long hair slicked back in a ponytail, was a massive and intimidating man. He turned his muscular torso to study the two men before grunting in response. His disapproval was apparent.

It was normal for him to disagree with anything Kyle suggested. Carlos was suspicious of anyone not Guatemalan, let alone his direct competition for Jose's coveted top lieutenant. Kyle never turned his back on him whenever possible. They were fairly equal in strength, but the other man was ruthless. The scar he bore across his right brow matched the cruelty inside. Nothing was considered taboo for him if it meant he would get what he wanted. Kyle was surprised he hadn't found himself the victim of an *accident* yet. Much like the storm around them, the tension between the two men was also growing. One of them would be dead soon if Kyle didn't get out.

It sure as hell isn't going to be me, he thought to himself as he and Carlos shared a look.

Kyle grabbed for the radio mounted on the wall near him. "I'll try to reach Chang or Ricky," he said to Jose. Ricky was the newest member of the small group that had come south for the endeavor and was staying at Felipe's house. Neither man was expecting to hear from them now, so Kyle was unsure as to whether or not he would get through.

As Carlos went to work trying to turn the nose of the boat, a loud explosion erupted from deep in the vessel. A billow of smoke crept up the stairs almost instantly, and the other two men on board ran up coughing and gagging.

"What the hell was that?" Jose called, trying to walk towards the men. "What did you two idiots do!"

"It was one of the pumps," Kyle explained as the two gasped for air. He knew the pumps were already being pushed past their limits. "It burned up." He turned back to the radio and began speaking into it more urgently, switching to another channel.

"Yes, the pump," Fredrick, the smaller of the two, said hoarsely. "The boat is on fire!"

"Oh, don't worry; the water will put it out," Kyle said sarcastically. "It should start rising very quickly now."

Jose looked at him incredulously.   "You mean we

really are going to sink?" he asked quietly, his voice barely audible above the storm.

"Yes," Kyle answered matter-of-factly. "The other pump will only buy us a few minutes. I can't raise anyone," he added, throwing the handset down. He stumbled over to the other wall and looked intently at the map fastened to it. Quickly looking at their present coordinates, he traced their location and hunted for a body of land. He didn't see anything closer than a couple hours away in good weather. They didn't have two hours. The lifeboat on board wouldn't last long in these waves. Unless there was something close by, they were all dead.

"Felipe!" Kyle yelled. The other guy from below, still wiping at his eyes, hustled over to him and studied the same map. Although he was a member of Jose's army, he still resided in the small town they sailed from. Being a native of the area, Kyle was hoping Felipe might know of an island not on the older map. Understanding the question without having to be asked, Felipe looked through some other loose maps on the shelf in front of them. Finding the one he wanted, he opened it on the table.

"Here!" Felipe declared, pointing with triumph at a small dot. "This is less than half an hour from here!" he yelled with obvious relief.

"What is it?" Kyle asked, eyeing the map and looking for a name. There wasn't one.

"Who the hell cares what it is?" Carlos complained, already headed for the back of the boat where the life raft was tethered. "Get the rifles," he told Felipe.

"Come on!" Jose ordered Kyle. He was balanced at the head of the stairs leading down to the belly of the boat. "We've got to get the money!"

Kyle followed him down the stairwell that now smelled of burnt machinery. Smoke hung in the air, and he squinted against the tears that sprang to his eyes as he stepped down into about two feet of water at the bottom. Jose disappeared into the first cabin on the right. Kyle's own quarters were at the end of the short hall. If he tried to get the SAT and was caught, which was likely, he would be dead. If he didn't get it, he would be unable to call his contact, leaving him on his own. What was the likelihood of him taking down the Chinese dealer *and* Jose's group? He didn't care for the odds. As he went past the first cabin and headed down the hall, Jose suddenly appeared at the door.

"What the hell are you doing?" he demanded.

"I wanted to get my bag," Kyle explained, keeping his expression neutral. The other man eyed him for a moment.

Just then, the boat tipped extremely to one side, slamming them both into the wall. It didn't right itself, and they both struggled to remain standing as cold seawater splashed around them. Jose thrust one of the two heavy duffels he was carrying out to Kyle.

"Forget your bag!" he yelled, turning back to the now-sideways stairs.

The boat groaned in protest and seemed to settle further, prompting Kyle to follow him. There wasn't any time to send out a distress call now; not that Jose would permit it. He was a wanted man. As Kyle reached the deck and made his way to the life raft, a leaden weight settled into his stomach.

Seven

Kyle
Sunday, 9:00 P.M.

Another wave slammed into Kyles back, knocking him to his knees in the sand as it washed over him. Fighting furiously against the churning blackness, he came up gasping as the water surged back out to sea, trying to pull him with it. Disoriented, he struck out with both his hands and feet, trying to find purchase on anything solid. After a brief moment of panic, his boots hit the ground. Using what strength he had left, Kyle pushed himself upright and plowed through the thigh-deep water before it could swell again. Coughing out seawater, he struggled the rest of the way up the beach before finally collapsing beyond the ocean's reach.

After catching his breath, he turned back to the storm-induced twilight. Squinting against the torrents of rain and flying seafoam, Kyle searched for the other men.

The duffel bag Jose gave him was still slung across his back, and he hoped it was watertight or else someone would be spending a lot of time drying out all the money inside. He'd been tempted to shed the weight anchoring him down several times. But if he lost it, he might as well crawl off and hide in the jungle because Jose's fury would match the ocean.

He had already spotted Carlos' large form ahead of him as he was coming out of the water. Unhindered, the other man had an easier time of it. Kyle saw he was now a short distance down the beach, helping who looked to be Jose out of the thunderous breakers.

Taking another deep breath, Kyle managed to get to his feet and staggered towards the other men. Within a half hour, the three of them located Felipe and Fredrick, both battered and waterlogged. It was amazing none of them drowned. Fortunately, the lifeboat didn't capsize until they'd gotten into the breakers closer to shore.

Once reunited, they quickly determined which direction was south, and Felipe offered to lead the way. Yelling to be heard over the noise of the storm, he claimed to know where he was going. Walking hunched against the gale-force wind that threatened to topple him, Kyle wanted nothing more than to find some form of shelter against the tempest.

It felt as if they were trudging through the sand forever, but eventually Kyle could see a light ahead of them, illuminating a dock and a decent sized boathouse. The structures appeared to be standing up to the storm's beating.

A boat and electricity means some form of civilization, Kyle thought as they grew nearer to the light. *If they have a radio,*

I might be able to sneak in a call.

His spirits rising at the thought of getting another shot at a successful arrest, Kyle gathered in the huddle the men formed in front of the boathouse. The pole holding the light was bending so far over in the wind that it looked as if it might snap. Fronds blew past them as Felipe pulled on the door and discovered that, thankfully, it was unlocked.

The five men hurried inside the shelter, which turned out to be a cramped boathouse. The weathered and aging timbers groaned around them. Someone turned on a dim light, and Kyle saw a small cabin cruiser was securely tied down. It was big enough to carry them all back to the mainland, but not to get the weapons. They were picking up a dozen or so large crates that would have to be concealed. It wouldn't work.

Kyle's only hope was they wouldn't find another larger boat moored somewhere else. If there wasn't, it would force them to return to the mainland where he would have the opportunity to get re-organized. Otherwise, his whole plan was blown to shit.

Climbing onto the rocking boat, Kyle located the radio. To his dismay, the top was off and some parts were obviously removed. Despite its appearance, he tried turning it on, but that only confirmed the obvious.

"The radio is broken," he called out to the others, trying to keep the anxiety out of his voice.

"There's a resort up there," Felipe explained, pointing towards the vegetation outside. "They should have a phone or radio."

"A resort?" Jose echoed. "What else is here?" he demanded, his voice rising dangerously.

"Nothing," Felipe quickly answered, raising his hands in a calm-down gesture. He rushed to explain. "It's a private island. Some small rental cabins around the main house. Nothing else. There shouldn't be more than ten or fifteen people here at most, I would guess. We'd sneak out here to party when we were kids, back before it was a resort."

"When was the last time you were here?" Carlos snapped. He was clearly as unhappy as Jose at the thought of encountering anyone and having to explain themselves.

"Um, about ten years ago," Felipe guessed, looking at Fredrick for confirmation.

"Si," Fredrick nodded. "There's nothing else here," he said in Spanish, his preferred language.

Kyle's thoughts raced as he tried to come up with a plan that would prevent them from interacting with the vacationers. But they were already a few minutes late contacting the suppliers, and he knew that was Jose's only concern right now. There was no way he'd keep him away from a working radio, and Kyle knew the Guerilla wouldn't hesitate to kill anyone who got in his way. Hopefully, if the resort was still there, they evacuated everyone before the storm hit.

Visibly relaxing, Jose clapped and then rubbed his hands together. "So long as they didn't move the building, it would appear we are in luck, compadres," Jose barked.

Kyle saw the change in the other man's face even in

the weak light of the boathouse. He'd seen the manic excitement in their leader's eyes on many occasions. It was one of the few emotions he displayed besides rage and a sick sense of humor. He preferred the rage.

"Fate has given us another opportunity," Jose announced, heading for the door.

An especially fierce gust of wind struck the side of the building as if in answer to Jose's statement, followed by a large crash that reverberated through the floor. The room was plunged into darkness, enveloping Kyle and the other men.

The situation was getting further out of control, and Kyle couldn't see a way to stop it. Not without ruining years of work and likely getting himself killed, leaving the people up at the house to defend themselves. Now, not only was he cut off from his own contacts, but he'd also managed to get into a potential hostage situation.

Cursing silently to himself, he felt along the wall and followed the darker shadows of the other men exiting the building. As Kyle emerged into the gloom of the storm, he noticed an old wooden sign. It had fallen victim to a large mango tree that also tore out the power lines and part of the boathouse roof. Its white-washed lettering almost glowed in the shadows.

Carter's Resort
The last paradise on earth!

I hope you people have some better luck among you than I do, Kyle thought ominously. *Or else we're all going to find ourselves in hell instead.*

Eight

Chris
Sunday, 9:30 P.M.

It only took Max a few minutes to show Chris, Desmond, and David the correct functions and passwords needed to log on to the painfully slow internet. Desmond declined Chris's offer to let him go first. He then guided a stricken David out of the small room, explaining how waiting his turn was the polite thing to do.

After spending about a half-hour reviewing her email in private, Chris returned to the rec room. Her correspondence was the typical work-oriented follow-ups. Of course, any active cases had been passed on to another investigator, so there wasn't anything there she needed to see, but habits were hard to break. David almost knocked her over in his rush to the computer, his eyes wide and eager for the 'fix'.

"I'm surprised it worked at all in this weather," Max said to her, looking up from the pool table.

"It cut out twice while I was using it, and I had to log

back in," she explained. "It's a pretty long process to work the satellite uplink. I didn't get a chance to tell David, but I suppose he'll find out. Are you still letting Max win, George?" she asked sweetly, raising her brows.

George muttered something unintelligible, causing both Chris and Max to laugh. Just then, a loud and over-exaggerated moan came from the den as David discovered he couldn't log on.

"I'm sorry, David," Chris said to him as he emerged from the room behind her. "It dropped the connection a couple of times, and I was only able to get back on briefly. Maybe try again in a little while?" He looked seriously distraught.

Chris knew how kids, and plenty of adults, were attached to their electronics, and he was probably feeling lost without it. She was required to be computer and tech savvy for her daily work, but she was also from an era that could still remember what life was like without it. Sometimes she missed the slower pace.

"I should have let you go first," Chris told the teen. Crossing her arms, she studied him for a moment, the clinical side of her always curious about the thought and emotional process.

He was obviously trying to control his response. Doing his best to appear uncaring, he ended up shrugging with an un-convincing smile. "Doesn't matter," he mumbled, making his way back to the dartboard.

Desmond and Cathy were still deep into their chess game, seemingly unaware of the ongoing conversations around them. Chris admired the young couple's ability to be so lost in each other.

Sitting back down in the same inviting seat as before, she tucked her legs under her thin, tropical-print sundress and picked up the book she'd left there. The storm still raged around them and it seemed the wind was even louder. She couldn't imagine what a grade four or five hurricane would be like if this was considered a category two.

Despite several attempts, Chris couldn't get back into the novel. She was on edge. *It's just the storm,* she told herself. Giving up, she put the book aside and watched Ken and David. It turned out the teen was quite the dart player. According to the scoreboard, he was ahead of his father by several games. Smiling, his withdrawal from the internet momentarily forgotten, he retrieved his darts. Putting another slash under his name, he bowed to his dad.

"Don't think I concede so easily, my young Padawan," Ken said good-naturedly while bowing back.

David rolled his eyes at the Star Wars reference, clearly indicating that any coolness brewing was now destroyed. However, he took up his spot at the throw line and started the next match.

"Ha!" George shouted to Max. "Ya see? That game was *all* mine! Now watch out, 'cause once I get started, there's no stopping me!" He clapped Max on the back and began racking up the balls for another game.

"You!" he said, pointing at Chris with his cue stick. "Get ready to give up your title, because once I'm done showing Max here just how much of a shark I am, I'm coming after you!"

Smiling broadly, Chris batted her lashes at him. "But George," she said gamely. "I thought you refused to play me again."

"That was a couple of hours ago. Things change. Now," he said, laughing heartily, "don't distract me!"

Shaking her head, Chris watched Karen enter the room with a fresh pot of coffee. It smelled amazing, and Dorothy was right behind her with what appeared to be scones. But before they could offer the snack to anyone, there was a loud hammering on the front door.

"What the hell?" Max exclaimed before quickly crossing the room.

"We're all in the house," Dorothy told him as he walked past her. "Who on earth would come here in this?" she added, following Max into the hallway.

Everyone else crowded near the foyer, but Chris remained rooted to the chair. She had an unexplainable urge to tell Max *not* to open the door. Her anxiety grew to such a level that she actually started to call out to him, but she heard the door slam open in the wind. The voice of a stranger could be heard talking loudly over the howling outside.

Walking soundlessly to the hall entrance, Chris gazed past the other guests and saw a middle-aged Hispanic-looking man standing in the doorway. He was of average height but broad through the chest. She sensed this was someone who was used to getting what he wanted. Despite his beaten appearance, there was an authoritative tone to his voice. But most of all, it was his eyes. Chris was at least ten feet from him, yet she recognized the raw edge and coldness in his stare that portrayed something unexplainable.

She had tried defining it to new agents during training, but they never understood what she meant. Not until they saw it for themselves. It was the look of a killer, and Chris knew immediately that they were in trouble.

***

"They're going to use the radio," Dorothy explained to her curious guests while ushering them back into the game room.

After a brief exchange, Max was now leading the group of men to the radio room behind the main desk. Chris strained to see them as they disappeared, but she couldn't tell very much.

"They apparently got caught in the storm," Dorothy continued. "It's a miracle they didn't all drown! Max is helping them contact some friends."

"You mean their boat sank?" David asked excitedly. "Cool!"

Ken looked embarrassed and mumbled something to his son, who scowled and slipped his earphones back on.

"How did they get to the island? Why were they out there?" George questioned, the pool game forgotten.

Dorothy and Karen had gone back to their original task of refilling coffee cups and handing out scones. "I don't know," Dorothy replied as she buttered a scone for herself.

"I think at least one of them is a local, based on his dialect," Karen offered as she handed a steaming cup of coffee to Ken. "The man who did the talking is Guatemalan."

"They were in a hurry to use the radio," Dorothy said in a more subdued voice, looking first at George and then Chris. "I'm sure they have an exciting story to tell us," she added, winking at David. "We don't have any more beds left, but I doubt they'll mind sleeping in here tonight. I should probably have Esmeralda start some more coffee and go get them some towels."

Chris put out a hand and stopped the older woman from leaving. "How many are there?" she asked evenly.

"Five men," Dorothy answered. "They were very polite," she added when she saw the look on Chris's face, trying to be reassuring despite her own nervousness.

"Where's Rico?" Chris asked Karen.

"Uh, upstairs lying down. He didn't feel too good," she said, glancing back anxiously towards the hall.

"Go get him," Chris said quietly to Desmond. "Stay out of sight, though. Do you have any weapons?" she continued, turning her attention back to Dorothy.

"Just a couple of hunting rifles that are locked away," the older woman replied, flustered. "I'm sure there's no need for concern, Chris," she insisted while watching Desmond rise.

George was eyeing Chris suspiciously, rubbing the stubble on his chin. Desmond looked to Dorothy and then to Chris, trying to decide how to handle the situation.

"I think the man Max was talking to is dangerous," Chris said bluntly. "What *are* five men doing out in the middle of a hurricane? They didn't appear to be your typical vacationers or fishermen. I just think we should be cautious until we know they don't pose a threat to us. We're completely isolated right now."

"I agree," Desmond said. "Rico and I can stay discreet until we know more about these guys. I didn't like the looks of them. You and Ken should probably stay here with the others," he said to George. Ken and George both nodded in silent agreement.

Dorothy sighed and sat down, unable to dispute the logic of what they were saying. As Desmond entered the hall moments later, several gunshots exploded through the house.

Nine

Kyle
Sunday, 10:30 P.M.

Kyle watched stoically as Carlos fired another round into the radio and turned the gun onto the shocked older man who was helping them. Before destroying the radio, they were able to get through to a contact on the mainland. It was quickly arranged for him to bring another boat and supplies as soon as the weather permitted.

Kyle fleetingly tried to convince Jose that it would be in his best interest to avoid trusting anyone else. Wait for the storm to pass, go back to the mainland themselves, and allow him to discreetly get them back in business. But just as Kyle feared, Jose was not willing to tolerate the extra delay.

To make matters worse, they'd switched channels and managed to get ahold of the Chinese. They were, as expected, riding the storm further out to sea. Over much static and broken-up words, the gun-runners agreed to move the exchange back two days to Tuesday morning.

When the final coordinates were relayed and the radio destroyed, Kyle knew he was totally screwed.

"Thank you for the use of your radio," Jose said pleasantly to Max.

The resort owner had been listening carefully to the exchange and his expression darkened as it became obvious that the men were up to something illegal. He fought now to maintain a neutral composure and shake off the shock of the gunfire. The fact that Jose didn't feel a need to hide any of it wasn't lost on him and Kyle could tell he was struggling to understand what was happening.

Felipe and Fredrick had already left the room before any of the radio chatter, claiming to need a bathroom. Now, Max looked over his shoulder, nervous to have his back to the door. The man had good instincts and Kyle hoped he'd continue to keep his mouth shut.

"It would appear, though, that it is now out of order." Jose's smile turned to a frown and the look he gave Max left no doubt as to his intent. "What other means of communication do you have on this island?" he asked evenly.

Kyle noticed, to the other man's credit, that he did not back down from Jose. Once over his initial surprise, he seemed to have accepted the situation for what it was. It was a trait most people didn't have, and it might be one Kyle could capitalize on later.

"That was it," Max replied, gesturing to the ruined machinery.

In one smooth motion, Jose had his own pistol out and crammed into the soft underside of Max's chin.

"Perhaps I wasn't clear enough," he spat. "I asked you what other communication devices you have!"

Carlos watched the exchange with noticeable pleasure, pumped for some action after having fired his weapon. He bounced back and forth on the balls of his feet with nervous energy, his eyes wide and pupil's dilated.

Kyle's stomach knotted painfully at the release of his own adrenaline, and it was all he could do to stop himself from pulling his gun and putting an end to this madness. Except it wouldn't be the end. He was in no position to take out both men. By the time he surprised one, the other would draw on him. Then there was Felipe and Fredrick. They were going through the rest of the house. He could easily make a bad situation worse.

Blinking furiously and trying to stay composed, Max answered through gritted teeth. "I told you, that was it. The boat radio is in need of a part I have on order. It won't be here until the next ferry comes on Friday."

"Are you expecting any other visitors before then?" Jose questioned.

Max shook his head with small, careful motions as the Glock forced his chin up and back.

"What about a phone?" Jose demanded, unconvinced.

"Cell phones are useless out here. Our isolation is one of the reasons our guests come here. We could get one of those fancy satellite phones," Max explained hoarsely, "but we figured we didn't need one before, so why start now? Part of the pleasure of living here is the lack of such technology."

The gun was slowly removed as Jose studied him. Max returned his gaze, refusing to give into his fear.

"If I find out you're lying to me," Jose growled dangerously, "you'll wish you hadn't."

Max believed him.

***

As the last shot erupted, Desmond had almost reached the staircase. Frozen in alarm, he was just turning towards the sound when he heard someone barreling down the steps above him. Spinning back, he found himself looking into the barrel of a .45. Putting his hands up defensively, he slowly took two measured steps back as the stranger advanced on him.

Behind the gunman, Rico appeared at the bottom of the stairwell, and Desmond hoped for a moment that they might be able to surprise and overpower the intruder. But to his dismay, Rico moved forward with a shocked expression as Esmeralda and yet another gun-wielding Guatemalan followed them.

"Where were you going, Amigo?" Felipe asked Desmond, keeping the weapon trained on him.

"Just checking on my friend there," he answered lightly. Sweat broke out on his forehead as he nodded towards Rico. "He hasn't been feeling well."

Rico looked back at him quizzically, his brows

furrowed. Reaching out blindly, he pulled a sobbing Esmerelda protectively to his side. He had no idea what was going on.

"Let's go!" Felipe barked without further explanation, gesturing towards the rec room with his gun. Fredrick shoved Rico for emphasis, causing the couple to stumble further into the foyer.

Desmond turned around in time to see Max exiting the radio room with the three other men behind him. Two of them also had weapons drawn. Their host was pale and clammy, his normally confident demeanor visibly shaken.

"I swept the house. Everyone else is in the other room," Felipe assured Jose, making it clear that this man was their leader.

Desmond exchanged a knowing look with Max and the dampness on his brow turned cold. As they obediently walked back towards the rec room, the Marine had an unshakable feeling that he had somehow let everyone down.

Ten

Chris
Sunday, 11:00 P.M.

The silence that followed the last shot was complete. Chris reached instinctively to the small of her back, and a coldness spread out from her stomach as she remembered her Glock wasn't there.

Dorothy tried to run from the room, but George grabbed her arm and held her back. "What can you do?" he demanded.

She looked at him fearfully and stood, indecisive. Chris knew she must feel the weight of responsibility for all of her guests. Anger also flashed in her eyes, no doubt for the strangers who could so quickly destroy the sense of safety and peace she and Max worked to build over the years.

"We can't just stand here!" Karen sobbed, obviously worried about Rico.

Chris noticed how Karen covered her belly protectively with her hands. Taking the young woman by the shoulders, she coaxed her deeper in the room and carefully positioned herself between the expecting mother and the entrance to the foyer.

"Dad, what's happening?" David yelled, ripping out his earphones as his father put his arm around him.

"I don't know, David," Ken answered. "Should we make a run for the cabins?" he asked, looking to George and Chris for guidance.

"You all should go, but I can't leave the others behind!" Dorothy cried, struggling now to free herself from George's grip.

"Maybe they already shot them," Cathy whispered.

Chris looked at the young woman who had gone deathly pale. Her blue eyes were wide with shock as she stood nervously spinning the wedding ring on her finger.

"Stay here. All of you," Chris ordered, making up her mind. She had to get to the cabin and retrieve her gun. She had no idea what she was up against, but this could be her only chance.

"What the hell are you up to, Chris?" George asked as he helped a now compliant Dorothy into a chair by the fire.

"If I'm the only one to leave, the men might not realize someone is missing," she told him without further explanation.

And I'll have the element of surprise, she thought. Giving Karen what she hoped was a reassuring hug, Chris ignored the questioning stares from everyone as she ran across the room.

Approaching the arched entrance that led to the

foyer, she could hear nondescript voices coming from back near the sunroom and staircase. Quickly veering towards the front door, Chris didn't even look back. She was committed now. She crouched low, treading lightly between the chairs.

Halfway there, the voices suddenly got louder, forcing her to drop to her knees. Doing her best to disappear behind a potted ficus tree, Chris peered out and confirmed that Max and the others were exiting the radio room and meeting up with the others.

After a brief exchange, they moved as one towards the rec room. She had nowhere to go, and there simply wasn't anywhere sufficient out here to hide. Max was the first to see her, and one look at the older man's eyes compelled Chris to make a run for it. She managed to get her hand on the door before a heavily accented voice yelled at her to stop.

Slowly turning, keeping her hands out from her sides where they could be clearly seen, Chris faced the man behind her.

Desmond, Rico, Max, and Esmeralda appeared unharmed and were corralled into the rec room with the others. Two rough-looking Guatemalan or Ecuadorian men, both wielding guns, closely followed them. That left her alone in the foyer with the three remaining assailants.

The one nearest to her, she had already seen speaking with Max, and she assumed he was the one in charge. Behind him was a large man who might have been darkly handsome except for the raw, ragged scar that cut across part of his face and the cruel twist to his lips.

Leaning against the wall, as if bored with the whole proceedings, was the only white man of the group. Chris guessed he was in his early thirties and around six feet tall. His dark, shaggy hair was still damp and unkempt. He had a strong jaw covered with probably what was several days' growth, and his wet t-shirt clung to a broad, well-muscled chest. Despite his haggard appearance, his rough good looks were disarming. If it weren't for the lack of any emotion is his steely eyes, Chris would have thought him out of place with these criminals.

While he looked bored, the other larger man seemed to be having a great time. Leering at her, he looked her over approvingly and summoned her with his gun. "Now why would you want to go running out into that storm, Senorita?" he asked. "Come with us, we want to get to know all our new friends. Especially the pretty ones. Si, Jose?" he added, nudging the man in front of him.

"Focus, Carlos," Jose scolded good-naturedly. "We mustn't get distracted."

Taking hold of Chris's left wrist when she didn't move voluntarily, Jose yanked her roughly towards him, bringing his face within inches of her own. "Do what you are told, and your time with us does not need to be unpleasant," he said to her, the playfulness gone from his voice. "Comprende? Understand?"

His grip tightened about her wrist until it was painful enough to make her wince. They were about the same height, so Chris clearly saw the pleasure in his dark eyes at her reaction. Cursing herself for showing a sign of weakness, at the same time, she realized it might be to her advantage. The only chance she had of escaping this was to get them to let their guard down. To do that, they couldn't think of her as a threat.

Swallowing her pride, Chris looked down from Jose's eyes and let out a small gasp of pain and fear. Her shoulders sagging, she hoped to look defeated as she nodded her head in compliance.

"Good," Jose said, loosening his grip.

Carlos chuckled as Chris walked past him and back into the game room. She saw the other hostages, for that's what they were now, had been lined up in front of the shuttered windows.

Cathy was leaning heavily on Desmond, looking like a cornered rabbit. George was next to her with an arm protectively around the cook, Esmeralda. David was on her other side trying to stand nonchalantly, but Chris noticed he accepted the hand Ken placed on his shoulder. Dorothy, Max, Rico, and Karen finished the row. They all exchanged nervous looks, afraid to say anything.

Jose gave Chris a push towards the end of the line, and she went to stand next to Karen. The other woman took her hand, and Chris squeezed it, reassuring her she was okay. Except she wasn't. Nobody was safe.

It was going to be a long night.

Eleven

Kyle
Sunday, 11:30 P.M.

Kyle kept to the back of the room, quietly observing while trying to assess the situation. It was a good sign no one had been injured so far. If Carlos could be controlled, there was a chance they might be able to wait out the storm and leave without incident. So long as no one resisted.

Jose was a sick son-of-a-bitch, but he was dedicated to his cause. While doing a job, he was all business, withholding from liquor and whoring or any other distractions. He wouldn't allow anything to disrupt a clear view of his goals and quickly destroyed anyone he saw as a threat.

Felipe and Fredrick were strictly strong-arms and would only do as they were told. Carlos, on the other hand, was the wildcard. He did whatever the hell he felt like in the moment, without any thought of the consequences. It was the primary reason why he wasn't already Jose's second. It took a cool head at times, which Kyle possessed but Carlos did not. He was currently eyeing the tall woman with brazen interest, and Kyle sensed this had the potential of being a big problem.

The woman.

When he first saw her at the front door attempting to escape, he was relieved Jose only yelled at her. When she turned around, if it hadn't been for his years of practicing disinterest, he might have given himself away.

There was nothing revealing about the beach attire she wore. But even the loose clothing couldn't conceal her enticing figure. She was tall and lithe. As she stood there, her muscles tensed, and Kyle got the impression of a sleek cat ready to spring. Her long bronze hair and green eyes only added to the effect. At first glance, her soft, seductive features gave the impression of someone vulnerable, but Kyle sensed there was an unexpected strength below the surface.

Moments later, as he saw the defiance flicker through her eyes before she looked down from Jose, he knew he was right. He thought her timidity was an act; but fortunately, Jose appeared to be convinced by it.

Now, as he studied the strangers lined up before them and tried to decide who he did and didn't have to worry about, he wasn't sure where she fit in.

They had no way of knowing he was their only protection.

***

"Fredrick!" Jose ordered. "Take the bags and make sure the contents are dry. Then find a secure place to keep them." The other man took the bulging duffel bags and left without a word.

"I am sorry for disrupting your holiday," Jose told the group in flawless English. As with everything else, the commander saw his ability to speak English as a test. He rose through the ranks of the Columbian rebels because of his perseverance in every challenge he faced, and knowing the native language of his greatest financial resource was imperative.

"It was not our intent to intrude upon your stay here," he continued, pausing to look at each of them for emphasis. "We do not plan to be here for long. A boat will arrive Tuesday morning for us. You will have to sit tight until Friday. Max has told me that this is when the next supply ship will arrive. By then, we will be only a bad memory to you all. Now, it is up to you to decide how our time together will be." Although his tone was neutral and bordering on friendly, the gun he still held left no question as to the gravity of his statement.

"Look, there's no need for those," George said, gesturing to the weapons. "We'll just mind our own business until you're able to go on your way. We're of no concern to you --"

"I will decide whether you are a threat!" Jose interrupted. Taking a step closer to George, his sudden change in demeanor made it clear he wasn't to be challenged. "You see," he explained, his breath hot on the older man's face. "I have some very important people waiting for me. But because of this storm, I have to house-sit a bunch of tourists!" His voice rose in volume until he practically spit the word tourists with contempt.

"There is nothing I can do about the storm," Jose continued as he backed away without breaking eye contact. "But you!" Pointing a finger, he looked up and down the row of anxious faces. "I can and will control."

Kyle noted that while most of the hostages were looking anywhere but at Jose, the woman on the end seemed to be studying him intently. She must have sensed his gaze because she shifted her focus to him and for a moment, he was held captive by those green, smoldering eyes. She looked away quickly, but not fast enough. Kyle saw that, while wary, she wasn't afraid.

"To ensure that I feel you will cooperate," Jose was saying, "I want to know who you are. Since *you* are so eager to offer your opinion," he continued, waving his gun at George. "You may start."

George appeared unfazed by the leader's tirade. "My name is George Miley. I'm a retired brokerage dealer here on vacation from Canada. I really don't care who you are or what you're doing."

"You sure are mouthy for a money man," Carlos stated.

While his accent was notably heavier than Jose's was, it was still nearly flawless. Jose trained his upcoming general's carefully, and the fact that he had a gringo as part of his inner circle spoke to his sensible tactics.

"How do we know he's telling the truth?" Carols pressed. Grinning, he shifted the gun back and forth between his hands. "Maybe we should help jog his memory and make sure there isn't anything he's forgetting to tell us."

"Would you care to see my business card? I still carry them," George asked, undaunted.

Jose nodded slightly, permitting George to withdraw his wallet. When he pulled out the card, Carlos snatched it from him.

"It's legit." Carlos seemed disappointed when Jose grunted and motioned to the woman beside George. "You're next," he told Esmeralda.

The older islander leaned in closer to George and began speaking rapidly in Spanish. Kyle had no idea how her job as a cook would require such a lengthy dialogue.

When she had finished, Carlos was laughing. "Perhaps she could poison us, Si?" he quipped.

Jose moved on to stand in front of Desmond. The Marine stood at attention and, after a moment of tense silence, slowly looked down at Jose while visibly clenching his jaw.

Kyle closed his eyes, groaning inwardly. The kid's high and tight crew cut reeked of military, but he could probably get away with claiming any number of other professions. Or at least play down his role as a patriot. Jose might be smart and on top of many things, but he'd never actually been to the states. The only way he'd know the guy was --

"Desmond Laurent, United States Marine." The

statement was more of a declaration, spoken with force and an obvious amount of pride.

Kyle couldn't believe the man's stupidity. As he opened his eyes, he was already moving forward and frantically thinking of a way to salvage the situation. But he saw Carlos already had his gun raised and without even blinking, he shot the man in the chest.

As Desmond crumpled backwards, George rushed Carlos, who fired the gun again, knocking the older man back and off his feet.

In that instant, all hell broke loose and with it, any hope of getting off the island without a fight.

Twelve

Chris
Sunday, 11:45 P.M.

It was so unexpected that Chris didn't have a chance to react fast enough. While she figured Jose's response to the marine would be negative, the brutality of the other man was horrifying.

As Chris turned towards the falling bodies, she saw Carlos step forward to put a final bullet in George's head. She was two steps away when the white man intercepted and ripped the weapon from his hand.

Stunned, Carlos gaped at him, rage quickly building as his face turned red. "What the hell are you doing, Kyle?" he demanded, his voice dangerously quiet.

"Save your bullets," Kyle said evenly while squaring off with the larger man.

As they confronted each other, Cathy began crying hysterically over Desmond's prone form. Ken managed to roll him over only to find he was dead, probably before he fit the floor. The bullet must have pierced his heart because there was very little blood.

Ken looked wild-eyed at Chris as she kneeled beside him. He was paler than usual and making odd gasping sounds as if he couldn't get enough air. Placing her hand on top of his, which was still resting on Desmond's motionless chest, she tried to bring him back from the edge of panic.

"Breathe, Ken," she softly ordered. "Breathe. David needs you."

Ken gave a brisk nod in response and swallowed audibly. Nostrils flaring, he did his best to get a grip and slow his racing heart.

"Everyone else stay where you are!" Jose ordered when Max broke his paralysis and moved to help.

Chris had reacted without thought to the consequences when she ran to Desmond. Now she saw that Jose was eyeing her. It was disturbing how unconcerned he was that someone had been killed, another shot, and that two of his men looked as if they were about to rip each other apart.

She was furious. In all her years of investigating violent crime scenes, Chris never witnessed an innocent person shot and killed in cold blood. The blatant disregard for life sickened her.

Holding back her tears for the sake of Cathy and the rest of the guests, she turned from Ken. After giving the sobbing woman a squeeze, Chris shifted so she was kneeling next to George. He was conscious, at least, and struggling to sit up. When he faced her, he looked as mad as she was.

"It's just my shoulder," he managed to grumble

through clenched teeth.

"Maybe so," Chris countered. Grabbing a blanket from the couch beside him, she shoved it under his shirt and applied pressure to the wound. "But it's still bleeding a lot," she observed. Glancing nervously at the two quarreling men as the tension in the room continued to rise, she lowered her voice further. "You're going to need a doctor. Soon," she whispered.

Peering up at the man called Kyle, Chris wondered if he might actually have a conscious. It became obvious, however, that his intervention was more about saving supplies than their lives, as he and Carlos began arguing.

"If you've got a problem with wasting one of these American scum, then you're in the wrong regime," Carlos sneered as he grabbed for his gun.

Rather than surrender the weapon, Kyle pulled it away while shoving Carlos in the chest with his other hand. The two stumbled together the few feet to the wall next to the fireplace, the gun wedged between them. Cramming the pistol into Carlos mid-rift for emphasis, Kyle's face was still expressionless, but his voice dripped with menace.

"The reason why I've been so successful in fighting that government," he almost shouted, "is because I use my damn head! This," he continued, bringing the gun up and pushing the butt into the other man's cheek, "is all you have when the deal goes down! Your friend, Ricky, is gonna have to steal a boat for us. It took me days to secure an appropriate one legally. As a result, our contacts are played out in that small village. There's no way he'll secure us any weapons and there isn't enough time to have more brought in. So think about it." Tapping Carlos' forehead with the sights, Kyle smirked at him. "Who would you rather use this bullet on: a retired, injured vacationer or a dozen Chinese armed with semi-automatics?"

"It's not the Chinese I'm concerned about," Jose finally interrupted, watching the two men with amusement. "I know Chang. There shouldn't be any trouble. But Kyle is right, Carlos," he agreed. "Save your bullets. We must be prepared for the unknown."

Kyle hesitated just long enough to leave no doubt to his dominance, and then pushed off the other man. He held the gun out to Carlos, who took it without comment.

Chris guessed the man wasn't stupid enough to question an order from Jose, but Kyle's body language said it all. It wasn't over. While it might give her an opportunity later on, the fact that these terrorist were fighting amongst themselves made the situation more dangerous for all of them.

She'd heard enough to know they were Guerillas; of what faction, she hadn't a clue. Probably Columbian. This was likely either a drug or arms deal. The bands were usually comprised of fanatics and thieves, both willing to do whatever it took to obtain their goals of power and wealth, fueled by the rebel's rhetoric.

Chris had been starting to think it might be best to just sit tight and let them leave. But now it was apparent that things wouldn't be that simple. She made a career of studying criminals. She would look at all the evidence from a crime scene and try to piece together a behavioral pattern for the suspect. Most cases she dealt with involved a single individual. Whenever you had a situation with more than one person involved in the crime, it became much harder to predict what the next move would be. Chris found that to be the problem now.

Carlos would be happiest killing or beating them, while Jose preferred to sit back and control everything. Kyle was a little more difficult to figure out since he was so stoic. The other two men seemed almost insignificant and simply followed whoever was leading. But she couldn't count out their influence. With all of them in the mix, the outcome was unpredictable, and Chris didn't like that.

Now, with Desmond dead and George shot, there wasn't really any more deciding to be done. Any one of them could be next, and George needed medical help as soon as possible or else he could die too. Tuesday morning was thirty-six hours away, and Chris wasn't going to bet anyone's life on the odds that these men wouldn't self-implode by then. Besides, they needed to be stopped and put in jail where they belonged.

"I have nothing against protecting the cause," Jose was saying to Carlos. "Just be sure that if you feel the need to kill anyone else, you do it with the first shot."

"The only cause you care about is lining your own pockets!" Chris blurted without thinking. The complete indifference to Cathy's loss was more than she could stand.

She knew her reaction was nearly as stupid as

Desmond's, but at times her mouth seemed to have a mind of its own. It had gotten her into trouble on more than one occasion.

So much for playing the weak, timid woman, Chris thought sarcastically as all eyes turned on her.

"Stand up!" Jose ordered. Gone was the playfulness from before.

Chris slowly got to her feet. Jose took a measured step towards her, and as he drew within inches, the rancid odor of stale sweat and seawater assaulted her.

"Why don't you let me teach her some manners," Carlos offered, as he looked her over hungrily.

Jose merely raised an eyebrow in response, while still staring into Chris's eyes.

Was he hoping to see a reaction? He must not have gotten what he wanted, because he tilted his head up slightly and slowly grinned.

"Perhaps some lessons in … obedience isn't such a bad idea," he taunted.

Chris tensed involuntarily in anticipation of an attack. Glancing beyond Jose to seek out the scarred face of her potential adversary, she noted Kyle was positioned between her and Carlos. In spite of registering his presence, she was startled when he suddenly stepped past Jose and, without a word, grabbed her roughly by the back of the neck.

She gasped in surprise as his fingers wound through her hair, and he pulled her head back sharply. Grasping her jaw with his other hand, he forced her to look into his eyes.

Although Chris was caught off guard by Kyle's sudden lunge for her, she still reacted because of her training. Her hands went to his forearm, and she tried to pull free, but he held her fast, increasing the pressure on her face. It took all of Chris's resolve to hold back from defending herself. Her muscles were wound so tight they screamed for release as a sequence of counter-moves played out in her mind. But a voice of reason broke through, and she knew fighting back was pointless. Instead, she planted her feet, held firmly to his solid arm, and met the gaze of his cold, grey eyes.

It was how she imagined jumping off a cliff would be. Because she didn't so much look, as *fell*. The room faded away until all that remained where those eyes. Green flecks swirled in the grey, and in that moment, they weren't the cold eyes of a killer. It was almost as if --

Chris blinked … and blinked again, trying to clear her head. What was wrong with her? Was she so desperate for escape that she was already becoming endeared to her captor, like all those stories she'd read? Victims of Stockholm Syndrome were a personal interest of hers. She'd studied about the phenomenon at length. Surely, she wasn't becoming a victim already!

Re-focusing, Chris discovered the coldness had returned and wondered if she hadn't imagined the whole thing.

"Let me worry about this one," Kyle said gruffly. "Are you going to behave?" he asked, pulling her closer so her chest was almost touching his. "Or are we going to have a problem?"

"No," she whispered, not wanting to make a bad situation worse.

As abruptly as he had taken her, he let her go. She stumbled backwards but managed to stay on her feet, watching him warily.

Carlos moved towards her, but Kyle put a hand out to block him.

"I said I'll keep an eye on her," he challenged the other man.

Chris watched the exchange with interest. She now seemed to be a pawn in their power-struggle. Chris hoped losing one standoff that evening was enough for Carlos, and that he wouldn't risk another. Of the two, she'd take her chances with Kyle.

To her relief, Carlos shrugged and waved her off. "I think this one would be more trouble than she's worth. I'd end up wasting another bullet," he added, laughing at his own joke.

"Tell me who you are," Jose said without preamble.

Chris knew before Desmond and George had been shot that she would have to lie about her profession. The killing only confirmed it. She didn't think any of them would hesitate to 'waste' their ammo on a cop. Or at least make good on their other threats, something that may happen regardless of who she was. "My name's Chris Echo. I'm a journalist," she answered evenly.

"What kind of journalist?" Kyle asked.

He looked at her now with a dull curiosity, the fire from moments ago gone. She suspected his emotions were tightly controlled and only released when needed, as in his confrontation with Carlos. Even then, it was carefully calculated.

"I write for a travel magazine," she answered. "Actually, that's why I'm here, but the Carter's didn't know it. I've found it's a much more accurate account if the hosts treat you like a regular guest."

Fredrick walked back in from the room adjacent to theirs, taking in the scene. "It's all dry," he said to Jose, ignoring the body. "I've got it put somewhere safe."

"What's in there?" Jose asked, gesturing at the open door at the back of the room.

"Just an office," Fredrick answered and then continued the conversation in Spanish.

"He needs a doctor," Esmeralda pleaded to Chris while the men's attention was elsewhere.

Chris knelt back down beside George, where Esmeralda had taken over pressing on the wound. "They don't care," Chris told her matter-of-factly. "Even if we could call for help or leave at will, the storm would prevent both for probably another twenty-four hours, if what Max said about it is accurate."

Cathy had stopped sobbing but was still moaning quietly while stroking Desmond's hair. Ken's breathing was back to normal, and he had an arm around her. The rest of them looked on helplessly, afraid to move for fear of the gun Felipe held on them steadily.

"I want you to go back to the boathouse," Jose was saying to an unhappy Fredrick. "Disable the boat. Permanently. Come Tuesday morning, I don't want anyone leaving this island besides us."

Chris was dismayed when Jose gave the order to destroy the boat. But she was still encouraged that they failed to recognize the significance of the computer in the den. She breathed a little easier as Jose resumed his questioning with the next person in line without challenging her claim to being a journalist.

Now, she thought, *I have to find a way to gain access to the computer.* It was their last hope to get any kind of help, medical or otherwise. Chris was afraid that waiting until Tuesday would be too late. For all of them.

A strong gust of wind slammed into the house, reminding Chris of the storm still raging around them. Although they were inside and safe from its reach, there was nowhere to go to escape the nightmare they were trapped in.

Thirteen

Kyle
Monday, 12:00 A.M.

Kyle watched Fredrick go with unease. He silently struggled to find a legitimate reason to counter Jose's order. But, as with the radio, he was unable to come up with a valid argument for keeping the boat intact. The islanders couldn't be allowed a way to get off the island on their own. Unlike the CIA, who was after Chang, there were those in the Mexican government who would be thrilled to apprehend Jose Martinez.

The front door slammed open as the wind caught it and then again after a string of curses in Spanish from Fredrick. Felipe chuckled at the misfortune of his comrade but looked nervous when Jose turned towards him in response.

"Gather their belongings."

Felipe appeared relieved by the order and began to collect wallets, purses, and useless cellphones.

Kyle blinked slowly as he watched Felipe. It was a

distraction while he went over his options. Being out-manned and out-gunned, if he acted prematurely he could get himself killed and prompt Jose to kill the rest of the hostages. Without knowing it, he'd already come to the same conclusion as Chris. This wasn't going to end peacefully. He would have to take each man out of play covertly, when given the opportunity. He couldn't allow the situation to continue.

Although the removal of Chang from the gun smuggling empire would ultimately save hundreds of lives, he couldn't allow another to be taken here. He might be deep under cover, but there were limits to what Kyle could and could not participate in. Holding innocent, unarmed civilians at gunpoint far exceeded those limits, and he held himself personally responsible for the Marine's death.

Kyle realized, too late, that he should have stopped this on the beach. He, of course, had no way of knowing what was going to happen, but he might have been able to prevent all of this!

Closing his eyes for a heartbeat longer, he tried to rationalize his decisions up to this point. He had no way of knowing for sure that there was anyone else on the island until he got to the inn. It would have been crazy for him to try to stop them. The unpredictable nature of both Jose and Carlos made determining what course they'd choose even harder to define.

It doesn't matter what I should have done, Kyle berated himself. One man was dead and another seriously injured. He had to keep a level head and make sure he created the conditions that would allow him to carry out his plan. This meant separating the rebels and getting them alone. At the moment, there were three other men in the room with him.

When Fredrick returned from the boathouse twenty minutes later, Jose was done questioning the rest of the guests. Fortunately, it was without further incident.

"Take the body out back," Jose directed Felipe and Fredrick, waving his hand as if he were regarding a dead cat.

Cathy began to wail again as they pulled her husband out of her arms.

"Come on, Cathy," Dorothy cooed, wrapping the younger woman up in a tight embrace. "Let him go. Come by the fire."

Once his arm slid from her grasp, Cathy turned her head into the older woman's chest and allowed herself to be led to the couch by the fire. Sitting numbly on the edge of the cushion, she quieted down, but the blank look on her face was even more unsettling.

"You will all stay in here tonight," Jose announced, unmoved by the scene playing out. "You," he continued, gesturing to Karen. "Come here."

Rico stepped in front of his wife and glared at Jose. Speaking in Spanish, he offered compliance but made it clear his wife was off limits.

Kyle was relieved when Jose laughed in response. "Relax, Amigo." Turning to Felipe, who had just walked back into the room, he pointed now at Rico. "Take this hero and go get enough blankets and other necessities so our guests can be comfortable tonight."

His face flushing, Rico responded by walking purposefully from the room without comment, Felipe trailing behind him.

Kyle eyed the other men left in the room. Fredrick was stationed by the entrance with his gun out, eyes sharp on everyone's movement. Jose sauntered to the far corner, motioning for Carlos to follow him. The two engaged in a hushed conversation that was most likely about Carlos' friend on the mainland. Jose was all about loyalty, and their whole mission now depended upon a man he didn't even know.

Carlos stuffed his pistol back into the shoulder holster strapped to his broad chest so he could talk with his hands. Jose had already put his away. It was a good sign that the men were relaxing. Kyle figured he might be able to eliminate them before Fredrick could react, but that still left Felipe separated and with another hostage. The risks just weren't acceptable.

He determined all of this even as he began to draw his gun. It took some effort to slow his heart rate as he pushed it back into the drop-leg holster fastened to his thigh.

When Jose turned to him seconds later, Kyle only appeared bored.

"I think we should search the cabins," he said to Kyle. "Confirm their identity and make sure nobody has any phones or other gadgets that'll work out here."

Kyle looked at the walls around them that were protesting under the wind and rain. Although going out into the hurricane now instead of waiting until morning was unnecessary, it was typical of Jose. If he saw a potential problem, he took care of it. Now. Rather than trying to point out the sensibility in waiting, Kyle saw that this might give him the chance he needed. Whoever went with him could have an 'accident' on the way.

"You," Jose ordered, beckoning to Dorothy. "Come here." Since Karen had suffered the same fate without any intended harm, Dorothy left Max's side and timidly walked over to where the men stood.

"Tell me about the cabins," he ordered. "How many are there, and how do you get to them?"

"There are five," Dorothy replied quietly. "Three to the north and two to the south. The two trails are clearly marked."

"Good," he mused. "Kyle, you take the two to the south. Fredrick, you get the other three. Be thorough."

Before they could discuss it further, Felipe and Rico returned, loaded down with bedding.

"Help pass that stuff out," Jose told Dorothy, who was still standing by them uncertainly. "Then, I'm going to borrow your cook and find some food.

"Collect anything of interest," he continued to Kyle and Fredrick as he looked through the items Rico dropped on the floor. Finding two flashlights, he gave them to Kyle.

Fredrick mumbled his complaints about having to go back outside again, but not directly to Jose. As they headed for the front entrance, Kyle looked over the tired group of people that were trying to find places to lie down. Someone had turned the lights off, and the fire dimly lit the room. Chris was watching him intently, and it wasn't until the door closed behind him that he realized what it was he had seen in her firelit, green eyes.

Fear.

Fourteen

Chris
Monday, 1:00 A.M.

She was as good as dead. Chris hadn't even considered the possibility of her ID being found. The terrorists already collected their wallets, purses, phones, and other electronic devices they had on them. When it was announced that they would all stay there at the house until the group of men left, she'd considered herself lucky she'd left her purse behind in the cabin. It never crossed her mind they'd go looking for it.

Chris still couldn't believe Jose ordered his men out into the storm. It helped to provide her with a better understanding of whom she was dealing with. He was so focused on completing his task that he wasn't even rational. When Jose found out what her true profession was, she had no doubt he would quickly and permanently eliminate her.

Chris knew Kyle wouldn't take much longer. He'd been gone for over half an hour already. If she was going to make a move for the computer, it would have to be in the next few minutes.

Fifteen minutes after the two men left, Jose took Esmeralda and Carlos to go raid the kitchen. Felipe was left behind to stand guard at the entry of the recreation room. The guerrillas were clearly unconcerned about the vacationers forming an uprising and felt that one armed man was enough to keep them in check. It was likely the only window of opportunity Chris was going to get.

Karen and Dorothy were still trying to console Cathy while she sat whimpering and staring into the fire. They draped a blanket around her shoulders and whispered to her quietly, but she didn't seem to be aware of their presence.

Chris and Max knelt beside the other couch, where George lay pale and weak. Rico and Ken were talking in low voices near the pool table, stealing furtive glances towards their guard. It sounded like they were trying to determine which cartel their kidnappers belonged to, and Chris was mildly curious as to how Ken even knew about them. David was uncharacteristically quiet, staying close to his father and looking very young.

"Do you think he's going to be okay for a couple of days?" Max asked Chris anxiously.

"I can hear you," George said, opening his eyes. "I'll be just fine. But I'm afraid the pool game's gonna have to be called a forfeit."

The bullet went through his shoulder cleanly, but he lost a lot of blood. Trying to smile, Chris gently squeezed his uninjured right arm. "Don't worry about it, George.

You'll just have to demand a rematch."

Too tired to respond, he merely grinned and slowly closed his eyes again. His breathing slowed, and he fell back into a restless, pain-induced sleep.

Convinced he was really out, Chris looked back up at Max. Her lips drawn into a thin line, she slowly shook her head. "He should make it alright for a few days, so long as he doesn't get an infection."

"If those son-of-a-bitches would let me get my first aid kit, I could at least sterilize the wound and give him some pain killers," Max said angrily. "We keep a fairly robust collection of medication since we're so isolated. I might even have some antibiotics that aren't out of date. You can buy pretty much anything on the mainland." Dropping his gaze back to the moaning man, his brows furrowed. "That Carlos fellow just laughed at me when I asked him!"

Chris looked warily towards Felipe, hoping Max's outburst wouldn't draw his attention. She was relieved to see that he was turned sideways, leaning against the archway. His focus, at the moment, was on his gun which he seemed to be closely inspecting and attempting to blow water out of.

Now was her chance. Kyle could be back any minute, undoubtedly rushing to tell Jose what he discovered in her bag.

"I'm going for the computer," Chris said to Max, surprising him.

"Now?" he questioned. "Why risk it? Wait until they leave and use it then."

Impatient to go, Chris hurriedly explained. "Half a day could mean George's life," she stated. "But what's more important is the very strong possibility that when they leave Tuesday, they'll have decided that allowing any of us to live is too much of a risk."

Max rubbed his hands together nervously. He must have considered that scenario himself, but having her second the notion made it seem more likely.

Edging slowly backwards on the floor, while keeping an eye on Felipe, Chris delivered her final motivation. "There's also a very good chance I won't be alive in another ten minutes. I don't have time to explain," she whispered to the confused man. "But I have contacts I can email who will be able to immediately send the appropriate kind of help."

Reaching George's feet, she went to her hands and knees and crawled across the space to the other couch where the three women sat. Dorothy and Karen looked at her with surprise, but said nothing when Chris motioned for them to be silent.

Edging around the large piece of furniture, she estimated there was an open span of about fifteen feet to the den door. Fortunately, the pool table was centered in it.

Glancing once more at Felipe, who was on the far side of it and still distracted, she quickly crawled across the floor, using the pool table as a cover. Rico and Ken watched her with interest but, to their merit, didn't react.

Relieved to reach the darkness of the smaller room, Chris paused to take a deep breath and sprinted to the computer.

Fifteen

Kyle
Monday, 12:30 A.M.

The wind nearly knocked Kyle off his feet when he stepped out from the porch. Tucking his head, Fredrick grabbed one of the flashlights from him and saluted a farewell before heading up the dark trail on his right, to the north.

Turning to his left, Kyle staggered over to the trailhead and took shelter in the leaning trees. The wind-driven rain made it hard to breathe, and even in the jungle, it was a challenge to keep his eyes open.

He would skip going through the houses all together, but if he didn't show up with the expected personal items, Jose would be pissed. He needed to avoid that. While he only had two cabins to search, Fredrick had three to go through. And according the owner, Dorothy, they were also bigger. Kyle figured he should be able to finish well ahead of him. Then, he'd double back and wait for him at some point on the other trail.

He was confident in his ability to overtake him, especially when he'd have the advantage of surprise. Kyle was hoping to find a rope or something else he could use to tie Fredrick up. He would avoid killing him if possible. His goal all along was to hit each of the criminals with a long list of charges when the charade was over. Both Kyle and the US Government wanted to make an example of them to the other cartels. That would be hard to do if they were dead.

His plan was very simple. When Fredrick failed to return to the house, he would offer to take Felipe and go look for their missing friend. Once away from the Inn, Kyle would subdue Felipe also and then try to sneak up on Carlos and Jose.

While he believed he could restrain the two smaller men individually, he saw no way around a gunfight when it came to the other Guerrillas. Kyle knew it wasn't a great course of action, where any number of things could go wrong, but he might not have another opportunity. Jose appeared to be settling into their new accommodations, but the man was insane and could spin on a dime.

Turning on the flashlight he held close to his chest, Kyle hurried down the path. He was already thoroughly soaked, but at least the wind and rain wasn't as bad in the protection of the dense foliage. The waving jungle around him caused the shadows to jump and leap in the weak beam of light ahead of him. He couldn't shake the image that he was in a dark tunnel of tortured souls that were screaming and trying to claw their way in.

Relief washed over him when a small cabin suddenly appeared, backlit by an intense flash of lightening. It appeared intact. But his respite was short-lived as he rounded the corner of the building and the full force of the hurricane slammed into him. There was nothing between the cabin and the ocean but sand, and Kyle would have bet that all of it was being blown into him. His eyes were filled with it before he could close them, and he fell to the rough, wooden planks of the porch. Crawling across it, he thought he'd be blown away before finding the door, but he managed to open it, get inside, and shut it again before it had a chance to be torn from its hinges.

Hair plastered to his cheeks and neck, Kyle found the bathroom and did his best to flush the sand out of his burning eyes. Grabbing a towel, he wiped at his face and hair. His eyes were still watering, but at least he could see.

Moving quickly into the only bedroom, he pulled a lone suitcase out of the closet. Based on the women's clothing that was hung up, he guessed this was Chris's cabin.

Setting the bag on the bed, Kyle began pulling things out, eager to finish. He'd withdrawn two novels and a large beach towel when he froze. He couldn't be seeing what he thought he saw. Tucked under the towel and snapped into its holster, was an impressive, stainless steel, wood-handled Kymber 1911 .45. He stood there, staring at it dumbly. How could she have gotten the pistol through customs? Even as he asked himself the question, he saw the black wallet next to it. Flipping it open, Kyle saw the CSI, Seattle PD insignia, right next to Chris Echo's picture.

In that instant, everything changed.

She could just be on vacation, he thought, turning the ID over in his hands. No. That just didn't make sense. Why go through the hassle of bringing the gun? Kyle knew what a mess the paperwork was.

Her cover story of writing a review of the resort could really be just that, a cover. The Carter's appeared somewhat surprised when she revealed it, but none of the other guests seemed to expect her to say anything different. And no one showed any signs of looking to her for guidance when the shit hit the fan, which would have been natural if they knew she was a cop.

No, he figured she was probably investigating either the Carter's or one of the guests. That would mean she'd have to be able to check in with someone and give reports. Obviously, the radio wouldn't provide the privacy needed, so she must have brought something with her.

After thoroughly searching the cabin, Kyle had to admit that if she *did* bring a SAT phone, it was well hidden. Time was speeding by, and if he was going to head off Fredrick, it would have to be soon.

The only devices she had were a laptop and a regular cell phone, but there was no Wi-Fi available and she didn't seem to have any other special means for internet access. Of course, he could be wrong, and she might not even be on assignment, which would leave nothing to find. The only way to know was to ask her.

Fronds whipped the back wall and raked across the roof of the cabin. Looking at his watch, Kyle stood indecisively next to the bed. Running both hands through his damp, gritty hair, he stared at the shuttered window, searching for an answer.

He wasn't alone anymore, which meant he didn't need to take as many chances. Not right away, at least. Not until he got Chris Echo alone and determined what they could accomplish together.

Making up his mind, Kyle hid the ID and cut one of Chris's belts, using it to fasten her gun holster around his ankle. He would let Fredrick go. If there was any way to keep these people safe and still possibly salvage his mission, he couldn't risk it by acting prematurely.

Grabbing the wet hand towel he'd thrown down, Kyle stepped out onto the porch and held it over his face. Picking his way carefully down the steps, he fought to keep his footing and started toward the other cabin a short distance down the beach.

Once in the small structure, it only took a couple of minutes to discern that it belonged to the Marine and his young wife. Giving it a cursory glance, Kyle then rushed back to the jungle trail.

He was eager to return, feeling a new sense of purpose that had evaded him for far too long.

***

Felipe was the only gunman around when he got back. Seemingly content to toy with his weapon, he apparently didn't notice Chris's absence. Kyle, on the other hand, immediately determined she wasn't in the recreation room. Crossing the space to check the den, he passed by Felipe, who watched him go with disinterest. Max started to stand to block his way as Kyle approached him. The simple gesture of moving his hand to his gun made the older man pause. He looked into Kyle's steely eyes and slowly sat back down, obviously torn between action and fear of making things worse.

Sliding silently into the room, Kyle stood frozen just inside the doorway, watching Chris at the computer. As soon as he saw her there, he knew what she was attempting to do.

After several long minutes, Kyle felt nearly as frustrated as Chris must have at the signal's inability to penetrate the storm. Although he was excited by the discovery of the computer, he knew they were in a very dangerous situation. If it wasn't useful to them now, he had to get her to turn it off. Quickly.

As he took a step towards her, Kyle suddenly sensed, more than saw, movement to his left. Glancing back, he discovered it was Jose. He would kill her.

Acting out of instinct, Kyle drew his gun and rapidly shot off a round towards Chris.

Sixteen

Chris
Monday, 1:15 A.M.

Chris sat poised in front of the computer, her face washed in blue light as she leaned close to the screen. It wasn't working. After taking it through another reconfiguration process for the GPS and SAT set-up, she tapped in the password for the fifth time. She swore under her breath as the 'no signal found' flashed on the screen.

She didn't know what else she could try. Her only hope was that she'd get another shot at it later, after the storm died down. If she was still alive.

One more time, Chris thought, starting the process over again.

She heard the footsteps behind her but didn't even have a chance to react before the computer tower to her left suddenly exploded. As she threw herself back from the desk, she realized someone was shooting at her.

The chair she'd been on toppled over as Chris spun

to face her assailant. Kyle was already rushing her, and there was no place to go.

Without any time to counter him, the breath was nearly knocked from her as he slammed into her and literally threw her against the wall. He held her there, pinning her shoulders.

Chris knew fighting him was a lost cause, but that had never stopped her before. Bringing her arms up through his, she forced them out, breaking his hold. In one fluid motion, she grabbed the back of his head and pulled it down into her rising knee. The impact was solid, and knowing this might be her only chance, she went for his gun.

She hadn't hurt him as much as she thought, though. His right hand closed roughly over her left as she grabbed for the weapon strapped to his thigh. With his free hand, he landed a blow to her stomach.

This time she did lose her breath and fell to her knees, bile rising in her throat. Not giving her a chance to recover, Kyle lifted her from the floor as if she were a child and once again pinned her to the wall.

Looking up to meet his gaze, she expected to see a mixture of rage and possibly lust, but to her complete surprise, she saw regret instead. As Jose stepped in close behind him, Kyle looked at her almost pleadingly.

"Just shoot the bitch and forget about wasting the damn bullets," Carlos suggested from the doorway. He was holding a large sandwich, half of it eaten.

"No," Kyle answered huskily. "That would be too easy. I have other plans," he explained, pressing his body more firmly against hers.

He had both her wrists locked in his hands over her head, his knee wedged between her legs. His hip ground painfully into her own, successfully holding her in place. Chris tried not to notice the hard muscles of his body and the fiery trail his touch left in its wake. Her own body's betrayal infuriated her, but she saw, with some satisfaction, that blood was seeping from his nose and mouth.

"What was she doing?" Jose demanded.

Chris saw that the leader's gun was drawn and realized Kyle was most likely the only thing preventing him from killing her in that moment.

"I watched her for a bit," Kyle explained, his mouth inches from her own. He continued to stare at her as he spoke to Jose. "I think she thought the computer would have Internet capabilities, but from what I saw, it didn't.

"Why the hell didn't you check it out earlier, Felipe?" Kyle asked, looking off to his right at the doorway.

Felipe now stood behind Carlos, eyeing the sandwich hungrily. He shrugged slowly, unconcerned with his mistake. "I didn't think it was possible out here," he said lamely while pointing at the smoldering hard-drive.

"Who had her cabin?" Jose continued, ignoring Felipe. His gun was still held at his side. In his mind, the computer was no longer an issue. "I don't recall ever seeing a journalist fight quite like that." He grinned slightly at his last comment, amused again.

"I got it," Kyle answered. He looked back at Chris with a burning intensity. "She was telling the truth. She's just a writer. I found some of her articles."

"I've never seen you … *entertain* yourself with a woman during our time together, Kyle." Jose was glaring hard at the other man.

Snorting, Kyle turned only slightly so he could look at Jose, still positioned behind him. "You know how I feel about mixing business with pleasure. It's a dangerous distraction.

"My *interest*," Kyle continued, turning back to Chris, "is due to some very interesting correspondence I found on her laptop. Our new friend here is worth a lot of money. With some … gentle persuasion, I think we might be able to recover everything we lost due to the storm."

Chris managed to keep her expression neutral, hiding the eruption of emotions that Kyle's statements evoked. He had to have seen her ID and gun, plus he outright lied about the articles, computer, and money scheme. He had to have seen the signal failure message if he'd been there watching her for any amount of time. She didn't understand why he was protecting her.

Jose took another step closer to her, and Kyle almost imperceptibly squeezed her wrists, as if in warning.

"Where did you learn to fight like that?" Jose demanded.

"Self-defense classes," Chris said evenly, finally looking at the head terrorist. "You can never be too careful," she added sarcastically, struggling weakly against Kyle's hold to prove her point. "And Daddy was convinced I'd eventually be a victim. He'd pay *anything* to make sure I was safe," she added, focusing her intense gaze back on Kyle. If he wanted her to play the spoiled brat vs a trained officer, who was she to argue?

"Come on," Kyle said abruptly, pulling her away from the wall.

Chris stumbled into the middle of the office, her stomach aching. He pulled her after him without another word, still gripping her right wrist as they emerged from the den. While dragging her through the rec room, all eyes fixed on them. Max looked at Chris sheepishly. Ken, Rico, and David all stood with him as if they'd been talking and probably trying to figure out if she were still alive or not.

"No," Jose said loudly.

Kyle froze, causing Chris to crash into him. His muscles were taut, and she could feel the tension mount around her.

"You and Carlos have the first watch," Jose explained.

It was unlikely anyone else noticed the slight relaxation across his broad shoulders, but Chris still had a hand against his back from stopping the collision. She recognized the faint smell of nervous sweat and, in that instant, understood how dangerous the situation was for both of them.

Jose broke the spell by clapping his hands together once in a final dismissal. "When it is your turn to sleep, you can do whatever the hell you want with her."

When Kyle swung back around to face her, the only expression on his face was annoyance. He caught up her other wrist as if he was going to pull her in closer, and she instinctively tried to pull away. He surprised her by suddenly letting go, and she went sprawling into the stuffed chair directly behind her. Pointing at her with one hand, he wiped the blood from his face with the other.

"Behave," he said.

It was a threat … and a warning.

Seventeen

Kyle
Monday, 1:30 A.M.

Kyle felt sickened by the turn of events. He'd never hit a woman before, but if he hadn't stopped her, they might have both been killed. Anyway, his face didn't exactly feel great. He pressed lightly at his swollen lip and wiped the blood on his jeans. It was a small price to pay.

Dragging one of the extra folding chairs away from the chess table, he positioned it near the door of the den, where he had a good view of the room. So long as nobody else had any grand ideas of heroism, he should be able to keep everything under control.

A loud banging noise from the foyer announced Fredrick's return. He cursed as he fought to close the door against the shriek of the wind forcing its way inside. Moments later, he plodded into the rec room, soaking wet and in a bad mood.

"There you are," Jose said to him from his spot near

the fire. He was sipping on a fresh cup of coffee as if everything was perfectly normal.

The three women sat huddled on the couch where they hadn't moved for over an hour. George slept on the sofa across from them with Esmeralda close by, wiping his forehead occasionally with a damp cloth. The rest of the hostages, Chris included, took up the remaining chairs at the opposite end, closest to Kyle. They spoke in hushed tones, but were smart enough not to draw any attention.

"I was about to have someone go look for you," Jose chastised.

"You wouldn't believe all the shit I had to go through," Fredrick complained, drying himself off with a small towel. "They live in one of 'em," he accused, pointing at Karen and then Rico. "The other two were full of crap."

"Spare me your excuses. Just tell me what you found," Jose grumbled.

"Well, from what I could tell, everyone was being straight. But I found this," he explained, pulling an odd-looking cell phone from his jean pocket. "It's kind of weird. Looks a little like your SAT phone, almost."

Jose stepped forward and took the phone from him. "Whose is this?" he demanded, looking at the hostages accusingly.

"That -- that's mine," Ken stuttered.

David gave his father an exasperated look.

"Sorry, David. I swear I wasn't going to use it while we were here," he explained, apparently more concerned of his son's disapproval rather than Jose's anger.

"I promised my son I wouldn't work while we were here," he explained to Jose. "That isn't a SAT phone. It's a prototype. It's a new smart phone. It's more like a hand-held laptop," he rushed to explain. Ringing his hands nervously, Ken cleared his throat. "Look, you already know there isn't any signal out here. It's useless as a phone."

"Turn it on," Jose ordered Ken, shoving it towards him.

Ken took it and, after pushing the appropriate buttons, handed it back. Jose studied the display for a minute and then gave it to Kyle.

"Just like everything else here," Kyle said quietly, handing the phone back. "No signal. I don't think any of the phones they have would work until you're almost to the mainland."

Jose turned the device over in his hands and then flung it into the fire. "Just to be sure," he said to Ken, who watched it melt without comment.

"Max," he continued, turning to the other man as if a thought had just occurred to him. "Tell me, that computer of yours, did it have access to the internet?"

"No," Max lied, not missing a beat. "I've checked into it, but it's still just too expensive to get service way out here. We're alone on this island. That kind of costly setup can't be justified at this point."

Jose looked at him evenly. "That's good," he cautioned. "Because I am a man of my word."

Max recalled, all too vividly, the terrorist's threat

from only hours before. He had no doubt Jose wouldn't hesitate to follow through with it. While he'd been hoping to keep it a secret until they left, it was almost a blessing that the computer was destroyed rather than the truth discovered.

Looking at his watch, Jose set his empty coffee cup on the mantle. "I'm going upstairs to get some sleep," he barked to Fredrick. "I'll be in the master bedroom at the end of the hall. You and Felipe can fight over the guest rooms, but I want one of you sleeping down here, in case there is an issue. Get some rest," he directed as he walked from the room. "Your watch is in three hours."

"I'm getting some food first," Fredrick answered, walking past Kyle.

"Would you grab me something, too?" Kyle asked. Fredrick grunted in response and left for the kitchen.

Kyle eyed Carlos. The larger man had arranged himself in the entrance of the rec room. Straddling his chair, he glared back, leaving no illusion as to how he felt.

Feeling restless, Kyle got up and began to pace, sauntering past the front shuttered windows. The group sitting near them fell silent as he first walked by and then back again. He glanced occasionally at Chris, and each time she returned his scrutiny with an intense, unwavering expression of determination.

Three hours, he thought, forcing himself to return to his post.

The weight of the gun against his ankle was a constant reminder of Chris's real identity, and he would do everything in his power to get it back to her.

Eighteen

Chris
Monday, 1:45 A.M.

Chris watched with curiosity as Kyle settled into his chair and appeared to lose interest again. His expression was unreadable as he reached out to turn off the lights before crossing his arms over his broad chest. The room was plunged into shadows, making it nearly impossible for her to continue her scrutiny.

She was doing her best not to rub at her sore stomach. Being strong in the face of adversity was a trait she'd fostered for a long time, and for Chris, physical strength was a huge aspect of that. But remembering that, due to an odd change in circumstances, she was supposed to be playing the role of poor little rich girl, she allowed a small whimper of pain to escape. Seeing Carlos grin as he walked past her with a fresh cup of coffee, she even pushed gingerly at her abdomen, as if searching for a bruise. It wasn't *all* an act. She'd taken some hits in self-defense classes, but even though she was certain Kyle pulled his punch, she was feeling a little nauseous.

Max apologized to her profusely the first chance he'd gotten. Chris felt she owed him the apology, however, and couldn't stand it now as he said he was sorry yet again.

"Max," she whispered harshly. Looking to make sure Carlos was back on the far side of the room, she leaned in closer to the resort owner. "If I hadn't pulled that stunt, the computer wouldn't be destroyed."

"Yeah, and I'd be dead," he replied, looking over at Carlos and then Kyle nervously. "I told Jose that the radio was the only means of communication," he explained quietly. "He said he'd kill me if I was lying. It was only a matter of time before someone else besides that one moron saw the computer and asked questions. I don't know how you managed to convince them it wasn't connected, Chris."

"I didn't," she replied.

"What do you mean?" Ken asked. He and David were seated next to them on the floor, trying to distract themselves with a game of Uno they'd found. With the only light now cast from the distant fireplace, it was nearly impossible for them to continue.

David yawned sleepily beside his father, and it was obvious he was doing his best to appear unafraid. He looked younger than his fifteen years, and Chris felt a renewed conviction to protect these new friends.

She wasn't sure why she hesitated to tell them about Kyle's peculiar behavior. Maybe it was because she didn't yet understand it herself. Looking at the man in question, she found he was still ignoring them. His appearance gave no hint as to what he was thinking, offering no further clues to her questions. Until she knew for certain what was going on, she thought it would be best to keep it, and her identity, to herself.

Except I might end up needing Max's help, she mused.

One of the issues that had come up, in both her mandatory suspension after the shooting and her last meeting with her supervisor, Mick, was her resistance to working with other agents in the department.

Chris had a tendency to take it all on. If there was something she didn't know, she would take the extra time to find the solution on her own. For some reason, she saw going to a colleague, who may have answered it in five minutes, as a personal failure. If it were urgent, she'd bite the bullet and ask for help, of course.

The ultimate irony was that the one time she called her co-worker to ask him to help her, he ended up shot. To top it all off, he'd been hitting on her for months leading up to it, which she had adamantly rebutted. His bout in the hospital resulted in his ex-wife 'rediscovering her love for him'. Squirming a little in her chair at the uncomfortable memory of her visit to the hospital, Chris stopped rubbing her stomach.

In spite of the catastrophic outcome, she knew her supervisor was right. Chris had a hard time relying on anyone else. But there was a lot more than her ego on the line now, and she needed the help of someone who knew the island and the house.

Avoiding Ken's question, she turned back to Max. "I

need to talk to you," she stated.

"I still think we should just jump them while they're sleeping," Rico declared.

He was seated in the chair on the other side of Chris, sandwiching her between him and Max. She cringed at the tone of his voice. "Shhh!" she hushed.

"There are two guys awake in here with guns," Ken said to Rico. They had obviously discussed this earlier and disagreed about it. "How do you think we're going to sneak past them?"

"Well, we have to do something!" Rico argued, now whispering.

"We will," Chris assured him. She understood his need to protect his wife, as well as the place they called home. "But not yet. We'll have to wait for the right opportunity or else things will be much worse. Ken is right; we can't disarm them all."

"I know men like them," Rico said hotly. "They are a disgrace. And I do not believe they will leave us unharmed. I will die before I let them touch Karen!"

"I don't believe they will, either," Chris answered quietly. Rico seemed taken aback by her agreeing so quickly. "We won't let anything happen to Karen. But we have to be smart." Rico tried to argue with her, but she cut him off sharply. "No one else is going to die," she promised.

"Shut up, over there!" Carlos yelled across the room.

"I need to talk to Max alone," Chris urgently told the others as they looked nervously at Carlos. He had gotten to his feet and was watching them. Kyle, who was closer, seemed unconcerned.

After some hesitation, Ken ushered Rico and David over to the pile of blankets and pillows. They laid their bedding on the floor under the dartboard, leaving Max and Chris alone. After a few parting glares, Carlos sat back down, satisfied.

Karen got up from the couch and quickly walked over to lie next to her husband. Dorothy eyed Max questioningly until he motioned for her to stay with Cathy.

Chris waited several more minutes before turning to Max. The fire snapped loudly as it burned some sap, and the dancing flames caused shadows to flicker over his face. The opposite of David, he seemed to have aged considerably that evening.

"Who are you?" he asked before she could speak. "Don't try to tell me you're a journalist, either."

Chris looked down at her hands for a moment, smiling at his directness. "I'm a Criminal Profiler on a CSI team in Seattle, Washington." She whispered so softly that, even though he was inches away, Max could barely hear her.

He nodded, as if he had expected such an answer. "How come they didn't figure that out?" he asked. "Didn't you bring any ID? Are you undercover or something?"

"No," she answered. "Both my ID and personal weapon are in my cabin. For some reason, Kyle covered for me."

Max took a moment to mull over the surprising

information. "Perhaps he has his own agenda. Doesn't necessarily mean it's admirable or beneficial to us."

"I considered that," Chris replied. "But he also covered for you, Max. He's the one that told Jose the computer didn't have internet or satellite access. He had to have seen what I was doing, though. The signal just wouldn't go though."

"He might have thought that message meant there wasn't a signal to *be* found and didn't understand what he saw."

"That's possible," Chris agreed. "I imagine I'll find out when his watch is over in about two and a half hours, and we have our 'discussion'."

Max raised an eyebrow at her.

"He told them I was rich and that he has some idea to recoup the money they had invested in their boat that sunk."

Max leaned forward a little more, and his other eyebrow joined the first.

"No," Chris stated while suppressing a chuckle. "Another excuse Kyle made up. But I went along with it. He obviously wants to get me alone. Hopefully I can get some answers then."

Fredrick came back into the room and gave Kyle a sandwich before grabbing a blanket. Apparently losing the fight for the other bed upstairs, he looked around sleepily. Deciding on a spot between the couch Dorothy and Cathy were on and the den door, he was snoring within minutes of lying down.

"There's a small boat on the other side of the

island," Max suddenly whispered.

Chris thought he'd fallen asleep. She looked at him now with surprise.

He rubbed absently at the stubble on his chin. "I didn't want anyone doing anything foolish," he told her when he saw the look she was giving him. "It doesn't have a radio or anything. It's just a little fishing boat I cruise in sometimes. I figured we can use it to get George to the mainland after they leave."

"I'm afraid if we move him that his wound will open up again," Chris said pensively. "He's lost so much blood already, Max; he can't survive if he loses anymore."

"Then we can go and get help for him, at least," Max suggested.

"Yes, that's better than Friday, anyways. That's when you said the next boat is coming, right?"

"Right," Max confirmed.

"That's assuming we're still alive," Chris muttered.

The two of them looked at each other in the dimly lit room. Neither of them could think of anything positive to say.

"Why don't you tell me where the boat is. Just in case," Chris suggested.

The fire popped some more, and the shadows leaped as Max and Chris huddled closer together.

Nineteen

Kyle
Monday, 4:30 a.m.

Time went by at an agonizing pace. Kyle slowly ate the sandwich and tried not to look at his watch. Carlos, on the other hand, wasn't as concerned about appearing eager and constantly checked the time.

After the first hour, the whispered conversations around the room died off, and it appeared that everyone was asleep. Kyle finally allowed himself to find a more comfortable position. Sliding off the chair to the floor, he leaned against the wall and sat with his arms propped on his knees.

After watching idly while Kyle change positions, Carlos stood and stretched. Sitting back down, he caught Kyle's eye and grinned. Pointing at Chris's still form, he wagged his finger. "If you need any help with that wildcat, just let me know," he offered.

Kyle ignored him. He wasn't going to take the bait.

Carlos shrugged. "Fine. Have it your way," he said

coyly. "Just trying to be friendly."

They both knew what a joke that was, and it didn't warrant an answer.

The last hour passed without any further comments or sounds, other than the storm singing through the eaves and timbers of the house. Besides getting up to place another log on the fire, Kyle didn't move.

Drawing on what limited knowledge he had on hurricanes, he estimated the storm to be nearing its peak. Normally, they only had to deal with tropical cyclones, which were smaller versions of the monster currently engulfing them. Glancing out at the dim light spilling in from the foyer, Kyle figured the resort must run on a combination of solar energy and generator. That was the most common setup for these private islands, and it would explain why the power was still on.

Kyle listened to the howling wind and forced himself to stay sitting against the wall in spite of his nervous energy. Not acting wasn't something he was good at. Knowing he had about one day to come up with a solid plan and execute it, he was eager to *do* something.

He briefly considered his odds of successfully eliminating Carlos while he was the only other one awake. While he wasn't too sure about Fredrick and Felipe, he knew Jose would be sleeping with his gun in his hand. Being split up in different parts of the house actually made a direct assault much more difficult.

Tonight, Kyle thought. *If I don't come up with a way to somehow carry out the gun exchange while assuring the safety of these people, Chris and I will have to attempt a takeover tonight.*

We just need to make it through the day without another incident. But first, he had to talk privately with Chris.

After one more overly dramatic display of checking his watch, Carlos finally stood up, announcing the end of their guard duty. Walking the short distance to where Fredrick lay, he stood over the snoring man for a minute. Shaking his head in disgust, he nudged him with his foot. When this failed, he kicked him sharply in the ribs.

Fredrick gasped and rolled over, leaping to his feet with gun in hand. When he saw who was standing there, he slowly put the weapon away while rubbing at his bruised ribs.

"Why the hell did you do that?" he growled.

"Because you snore like a pig!" Carlos snapped, already turning away. "It's your turn to watch; and if I catch you sleeping, I'll slit your throat."

Kyle watched the men with a slight edge of amusement. He didn't believe Carlos would really do it, but he had no doubt Fredrick didn't want to find out.

"I need some coffee," Fredrick said while rubbing at his throat as if the wound had already been inflicted.

Movement in the foyer drew Kyle's attention, and he saw Jose and Felipe walk into the room. They were both bleary-eyed and frowning.

"I'll make the coffee," Felipe offered. "I can't drink the crap you usually come up with."

"Why don't we wake up the cook, Esmerelda, and make her do it?" Fredrick countered.

"Because we are men," Jose said, his tone dangerously low. "Do you also need someone to hold your hand on your shift? I shouldn't have to come down here to check on things, but this," he continued, pointing at Fredrick, "is why I am here. So get your freaking coffee, don't wake any of them up, and keep your damn mouth shut!"

Kyle resisted the urge to roll his eyes. It was the typical banter between Jose and his men, but he didn't have the patience for it right now. His anxiety had been growing for the past three hours, and he was concerned he wouldn't get a chance to talk with Chris alone.

Taking advantage of the distraction, he moved towards her sleeping form. While Jose just said not to wake them up, he'd already told Kyle he could do whatever he wanted with her at the end of his shift. Glancing at Carlos, he noticed the other man watching him with interest. If he saw an opportunity to jump in and cause problems for Kyle, he'd take it. He had to prevent that at all costs.

Twenty

Chris
Monday, 4:30 A.M.

Chris slept for maybe an hour and was awake at the first sound of voices. She observed the tense exchange between the men with interest. While they worked together, none of them seemed to be friends. That was why fascist groups never lasted or advanced very far with their cause. They claimed to believe in something as an excuse for their violence and criminal activity, but when it came down to it, all they really cared about was themselves and their own personal gain. Honor among thieves and all.

Still feigning sleep, Chris's heart began to race faster as she saw Kyle get to his feet and look her way. Determined to meet things head-on, she opened her eyes and pushed up onto her elbows. She watched him quietly as he picked his way around the sleeping forms and came to stand over her.

In spite of *wanting* to get alone with him, Chris still

fought the urge to flee as she stood up and raised her eyebrows questioningly. They needed to avoid a scene that could end up with someone else getting hurt.

"Let's go talk," Kyle ordered, motioning towards the hall with his head.

"Chris," Max said quietly from behind her.

She turned to him and gave a sharp shake of her head. He looked worried enough to do something in spite of saying he trusted her judgement, but he stayed where he was. Chris noted with relief that the others were still asleep. Her gaze paused on the form of Rico, one arm resting protectively over Karen as they slept. She was concerned about him. He was too eager to fight back.

Apparently, Kyle grew impatient with her. Grabbing her by the upper arm, he ushered her through the room unceremoniously.

Jose and Fredrick watched them go without comment. Felipe cut them off as he ambled past with the coffee pot, mumbling under his breath.

Stopping to avoid a collision, Kyle's grip tightened on Chris's arm as he turned her around to face him. She was acutely aware of their audience nearby when Kyle took her cellphone from his pocket and held it up.

"This one is yours?"

Glancing briefly at the unique phone case she had made from one of her own mountain photos, Chris met his hard stare and nodded. Was he going to make her unlock the screen in front of Jose and find something incriminating? She didn't have time to think over what sort of content they might find, before Kyle revealed the reason behind his question.

"Good. We'll use it to record your message. It'll mean more when your father gets it from your personal account."

Putting the phone away, he continued to lead her from the room. She noticed Jose nodding in approval as they left. Everything Kyle did, seemed calculated, and Chris was beginning to feel like a pawn in some bizarre game. One she didn't know the rules to.

Just as it appeared they would make it upstairs without incident, Carlos came up behind them as they neared the sunroom and stairwell. Kyle stopped to look back at him.

Crossing his arms over his chest, he took his time looking Chris over, lingering on her chest. "Remember my offer," Carlos finally said while smirking. "If you need help with your *interrogation*, all you have to do is holler."

"You'll be the first person I'll think of," Kyle remarked. "But don't wait up."

Chris had been trying to convince herself that Kyle wasn't going to hurt her. Everything he'd done and said until now had appeared to be in order to protect her. At the same time, she also realized that as far as Carlos knew, she was a naïve, rich journalist being dragged upstairs by a guerilla to be forced into making a ransom video and god only knew what else. Carlos' presence might be because *he* didn't trust Kyle's motives, either. Jose might have even sent him to observe their interaction. She shouldn't be going willingly. At least they were away from the rec room now, so none of the other guests would see it.

She'd have to act quickly to make it believable.

They were partway up the stairs with Kyle behind her, holding both of her arms. Quickly pushing herself back into his chest, Chris caused him to lose his footing. He had no choice but to let go of her to keep from falling. As she lunged up the stairs, she could hear Carlos laughing and Kyle swearing.

She'd just reached the second floor landing when Kyle grabbed her ankle and, giving it a yank, sent her sprawling. As Chris rolled onto her back in the darkened hallway, she experienced an unexpected flashback to her recent fight with the serial killer. During the one required consultation she had with the department shrink, she adamantly denied having any symptoms of Post-Traumatic Stress Disorder. PTSD wasn't an option for someone who believed they were always in control.

She was wrong.

Now, all the emotions from that fight-or-flight experience came rushing back, and Chris gasped, struggling to catch her breath as the rising panic choked her. Disoriented in the dark, she wasn't sure where she was anymore. But she knew she had to fight.

Scurrying back, she kicked at where she thought her opponents face ought to be. He expected it though and had already let go of her leg so he could lean back out of reach. Carlos was still laughing from below, but as Kyle stood over her, he didn't look amused.

Springing to her feet, Chris was still in the grip of blind terror and did the only thing possible. She turned and ran.

"Shit!" Kyle swore as she bolted. He hit the light switch beside him as he sprinted after her. Chris was quick, but Kyle was faster. She was almost to the end of the hall when his arms went around her waist, lifting her off the floor.

"Chris, listen --," he began.

But a hard elbow to the stomach cut him off. Raising her feet waist high, Chris planted them against the wall in front of her and pushed off. She was successful in throwing him off balance again, but he didn't let go this time. They crashed through the half-open bedroom door behind them.

Tumbling into the dark room, they fell onto a bed. Kyle quickly rolled her over, lying over her to hold her down. Light washed in from the hallway so Kyle could see the fear on her face as her heart beat wildly against his chest.

"I'm not going to hurt you," he whispered to her as she struggled to break free.

Chris squeezed her eyes against the wave of emotions threatening to crash over her. She recognized his voice. She *knew* it wasn't Martin Eastabrooke. She *knew* she wasn't back in her cabin, fighting over the gun that she killed him with. Forcing her eyes open, Chris looked up at Kyle in the dim light and tried to slow her breathing.

His brows were drawn together in concern. As he leaned in close to study her face, his eyes appeared caring rather than cold. The adrenaline brought on by her fear slowly ebbed and as she became rational again, she stopped thrashing beneath him.

"Good," he said soothingly. "You don't have to fight me now, Chris. There's no one else around."

She didn't understand what he meant by that, but for some reason she believed him. Taking a deep breath to further clear her head, Chris asked the one question she could think of. "Why are you protecting me?"

"I'll explain everything," he replied. "But first I need to close the door. If any of them hear me, we're both dead." He let this sink in for a few seconds. "Can I trust you to cooperate if I let you go?"

Chris suddenly became aware of how intimate a position they were in. His body completely covered her own, and they fit well together. An intense heat began to spread out from her stomach. Her pulse surged again, but this time for a different reason. His hair fell forward just far enough to lightly tickle her cheeks, inciting a strong desire to run her hands through it. Trying hard to ignore the sensations he was causing in her, she slowly nodded in agreement.

Kyle hesitated before pushing himself up, and she wondered if it was because he felt the change in her body. She had transformed under him from cold and rigid into soft and inviting, her face tilting just enough to expose the sensitive underside of her neck. She was thankful when he quickly rolled away. This wasn't the time or the place for it.

Flipping the light switch, he slammed the door and flung a vase from the nightstand to the floor. "You wouldn't give up that easily," he said to her when she looked at the shattered glass.

"No, I wouldn't," Chris agreed. Pulling her legs up under her, she sat on the edge of the bed, waiting.

Kyle walked over to her and sat at a safe distance on the other end of the mattress. He got right to the point. "I work undercover for the CIA," he said without preamble. "Together, I think we can make sure these sons-of-a-bitches never get the chance to hurt anyone again."

Twenty-one

Chris
Monday, 4:45 AM.

Chris couldn't believe what she was hearing. She hadn't known what to expect, but CIA? There were so many questions to ask; she didn't know where to start. Actually, she was so relieved that all she wanted to do was throw her arms around him and say 'Thank God'.

Instead, Chris gripped her hands together in her lap and tried to gather her thoughts. Kyle studied her as she visibly struggled to regain control of her emotions, and she wondered if her expressions gave her away. "What are you doing with them?" she finally asked.

"I've been undercover with Jose's organization for over two years now," he explained. "We're out here to purchase automatic rifles from a Chinese supplier named Chang. He's been my primary target all along."

"You mean to tell me you and your superiors decided Desmond and the rest of us are *expendable?*" Chris almost shouted as her face flushed with anger.

"No. And keep your voice down," he sighed.

"Then why the hell haven't you -- *they* stopped this?" she demanded. "A man is dead!"

"I know that!" Kyle yelled back, now equally angry. "I take full responsibility for what's happened. No one is expendable!"

"Then why haven't they done anything?" Chris pushed, lowering her voice as she realized they were both speaking too loud.

"Because there isn't any 'they'. I'm on my own. Do you really think I would have let this continue if I had any way of controlling things?" he tried to explain.

Chris's hopes were dashed as she realized what Kyle was saying. "You mean that when your boat sank --"

"So did my means for contacting my backup," Kyle confirmed. "They don't even know I'm here. I never had a chance to get the final coordinates for the exchange to them, either. Of course, that's not going to happen now. We'll have to stop them before then."

Standing, he began to pace the room. When he stopped to face her, she got her first real glimpse of who Kyle was. His expression was a mixture of conflicting emotions. "Chang will go free, and the last two years of my life will be for nothing. That's assuming you're alone," he added somewhat desperately. "I was hoping when I found your ID that you were here on official business."

"No," Chris said quietly, shaking her head. "I really am just here on vacation. Trouble has a way of finding me when I'm not even looking for it," she added sarcastically.

Feeling guilty now over her outburst, she looked into Kyle's troubled eyes. She understood his position was even more frustrating than her own. "I'm sorry I can't tell you otherwise," she said softly. "I'm also sorry for blaming you for Desmond's death. I'm sure you would have done something if you'd had a chance."

Kyle returned her gaze, and she could see the muscles in his jaw working as he fought to control his anger. "I didn't know what was going to happen when we washed up here," he explained. "I've been afraid of making things worse by acting too soon. If I ended up getting myself killed, and Jose felt betrayed, he'd likely take it out on you and the rest of the hostages. These guys are trained Guerrillas, and they know how to fight. We have to be careful."

Putting his foot up onto the bed, he raised his pants leg, exposing her gun. "This should even the odds a bit," he told her while unstrapping it. He sat back down on the bed and handed the gun over to her.

Chris was happy to see that he appeared to do things similar to herself. The sight of the gun lifted her spirits. "I really just want to go down there right now and start shooting," she said, taking her weapon. "Even though all my training has been that in a hostage situation, you reserve the gunfire for a last resort.

"Your training is right. If we leave just one of them in a position to fire back, someone else could be killed. That's not acceptable."

"So what do you think Jose plans on doing?" Chris asked. "I've been afraid he's going to see us as too much of a risk and just kill us all before he leaves."

"Not necessarily," Kyle replied. "So long as he doesn't have a reason to think of you as a threat, and Carlos doesn't get another wild hair. But I've been thinking about this all night. If you don't have a way of contacting the mainland, I don't plan on letting them leave. The odds of my taking Chang down by myself and surviving to get help out here afterwards aren't very good. If I'm on the boat when the deal goes down, Chang isn't leaving, one way or the other."

Chris looked at him steadily while mulling over all of the information. "That's suicide. You can't do it on your own."

"It doesn't look like it'll even be an issue. We need to take care of things here before Ricky arrives with the new boat. I can surprise him and secure it easily enough. The boat will have a radio, and he should be bringing a SAT phone."

"What if I *did* have a way to reach the mainland before then?" Chris interrupted, her voice level.

"There's a Naval Cruiser sitting out at sea, north of here," he said slowly while studying her. "They were going to make an amphibious assault in conjunction with the Coast Guard once I notified them. I could give you a way to contact them, as well as the coordinates for the drop. I found out last night that it's going to be about five hours from here, and four hours from the ship. Chang won't move to those coordinates until he gets the confirmation call from Jose on Tuesday morning. If he doesn't call as planned, Chang isn't going to wait around.

"But I don't see any way to complete the assignment," he said, resigned. "We're all stuck here, and my only concern now is ending this without any more casualties. I'm already going to be in a shit load of trouble for letting this develop. Plus, Chang will learn of Jose's arrest, and we'll never see him in these waters personally again. What a mess!" he exclaimed, getting up to pace the floor again. He rubbed at his eyes and pressed his temples as if suffering from a headache.

"There may be another alternative," Chris told him. Her mind was racing, and she had a plan. "There's a boat on the other side of the island."

Twenty-two

Kyle
Monday, 5:00 A.M

Kyle looked at her with astonishment. "A boat? Does it have a radio?" he asked, encouraged.

"No. It's just a small fishing boat, but it's a way to get to the mainland. I can send help for George and use my phone to email the coordinates for the drop to whoever you tell me to. By the time I return, you should be gone with Jose. Hopefully, I'd get the message to your backup soon enough. But you've already made it clear you're willing to take the risk."

Kyle was shaking his head. "The email isn't the problem. I have an address that'll work. But you disappearing would make Jose very nervous. It might set him off. The bigger picture here is that we have to weigh all the possible outcomes of our actions heavily. We have to choose the one that places the hostages in the least amount of risk, my mission aside."

"That's what I'm doing, Kyle," Chris persisted. "It

would be your job to reassure Jose. You'd have to keep the situation under control for just a few hours. He wouldn't have any reason to think that I wasn't simply scared and hiding out in the jungle," Chris argued.

She stood up and walked over to him. Gripping his upper arms, she tried to reason with him. "Think about it, Kyle. It's the best plan all around. You can even keep my phone with the ransom video. That might help calm him down. I could grab my laptop from the cabin. The ferry landing café has Wi-Fi. I used it before we left to come here."

Staring down into her flashing green eyes, Kyle found he couldn't look away. *She'd make a good interrogator,* he thought with some humor.

"What would be riskier?" she persisted when he didn't respond. "You and I trying to disarm all four of them before that guy Ricky gets here, or my taking a hike and a two or three hour boat ride? It's a way to get the help we need without a gunfight, *and* you still get a shot at Chang!"

He didn't like it, but she was right. He could see she was as stubborn as he was and wouldn't budge on her opinion. He grinned at her, and she seemed to realize she was still holding onto him. Suddenly releasing his arms, she took a small step back as he continued to scrutinize her.

He was slow to let the thought of successfully ending his two-year assignment sink in. As soon as Desmond was shot, all hope of that instantly faded. But it was gradually dawning on him. He might still pull this off.

His smile grew as Chris took another step back, looking somewhat perplexed at the change in him. "You wouldn't be able to go for a while still," he told her. "The water will probably be too dangerous until later tonight. Do you even know how to get to the boat? Or how to get to the mainland?"

Looking relieved that he accepted her plan, she went and got a box of tissues off the nightstand. "I think I can find my way. I went hiking on the trails yesterday. I just need to find the right one. Max thinks the water should be calm enough by midnight, although I'll wait until its light out so I can see where I'm going. He said there is a GPS unit on it with the mainland docks preprogrammed. I guess it used to have a radio. He took it apart to scalp the pieces needed to fix the one on the main boat." Walking back over to him, she pulled out some Kleenex and reached for his face.

"What are you doing?" he asked, amused.

"I seem to have done some damage," Chris said disdainfully.

Glancing over her head into a mirror above the dresser, Kyle saw a small line of blood trailed down the left side of his face from a scratch above his eyebrow. He watched her dab gently at it while trying not to breathe in her scent, a mix of sun lotion and musky sweat. There seemed to be a magnetic pull between them that he had to physically pull away from.

"I'm sorry about all of that," Kyle said as she stepped back, somewhat reluctantly. "I mean, what happened last night in the den. I couldn't see any other way."

"It's okay," she assured him, still holding the bloodied tissue out like his face was still there.

"How's your stomach? I tried to pull the punch as much as possible without making it obvious."

"I'm fine," she said quickly.

Kyle suspected she was lying, as she subconsciously rubbed at the spot. She looked almost startled when she noticed the Kleenex in her hand, and she bent to turn the garbage can upright before tossing it inside.

"I wish I could say the same for my lip," Kyle said lightly, touching the swollen spot. "If you hadn't put up such a good fight, I wouldn't have had to be so rough," he teased.

"Well, I guess being shot at and thrown around brings out the worst in me." Chris stared at the can for a moment before kicking it. It bounced off the wall and rolled across the floor. "It's been way too quiet up here," she said in answer to his startled look.

Walking up to her, he reached out and swept his arm across the top of the dresser behind her, sending several items flying. "Much too quiet," he agreed.

When she didn't make an attempt to move away from him, Kyle again found himself wanting to get closer. Much closer. Looking down at her full lips, he wondered what they would feel like against his own. He already knew what her body felt like, and the memory of her under him pushed out all other thoughts from his mind.

"I can't imagine what working for a man like Jose for so long must be like," she said breathlessly.

Her attempt at small talk was a clear sign she was

struggling to find something to move them past the moment. A sudden memory of the fear he'd seen on her face while they'd wrestled on the bed jolted him back to reality. His lack of womanizing while with Jose was the one aspect of his personality that *wasn't* an act. Allowing himself to get distracted in the midst of their current situation wasn't acceptable.

"I've only lived at his estate for the past year," Kyle explained. He kept his voice even with some effort, searching for the iron control he usually held over his emotions. "I started out as a simple contact on the American side. We would purchase his drugs and guns, putting them straight into evidence. We eventually traced the rifles to Chang and centered in on him. Jose took a liking to me, and when he invited me to go work for him, it was too much of an opportunity for us to pass up."

"What about your family?" Chris asked quietly.

"My marriage was already gone by then," he said reluctantly. "It didn't survive the first six months."

Chris was silent for several heartbeats, and Kyle could tell she wanted to say something: perhaps that she was sorry or she understood how he must feel. But she was intuitive enough to see he didn't want sympathy.

"How did you separate yourself from all the criminal activity? You can't tell me you've actively participated in this for a year."

"I've actually seen very little action," Kyle explained, thankful that she skipped any emotional pleas. "Jose has hundreds of men living in nearly primitive encampments doing most of his work for him while we live in comparative luxury in his million-dollar estate. He only goes out for the bigger operations, when he feels his presence will secure the profit. Chang surfaces a couple of times a year and demands a one-on-one with Jose. The last time we dealt with him, Jose left me behind, so I had to wait around for another four months to get in on it."

"What is it that you do for him?" Chris asked with obvious interest.

"Logistics. Most of it's handled via computers and other specialty devices, but some of it's still done by going to the right people and making a lasting impression. As a result, I spend the majority of my time on the computer and phone, making arrangements for drops and pick-ups. We take the occasional field trip to maintain our contacts and strong-arm reputation."

"I can't imagine playing a part for so long," Chris replied, studying his face.

He'd become detached again while talking about his position with Jose. Kyle re-focused on her, a small amount of warmth creeping back into his face. "It is a part," he agreed. "Like the lead role in a play, except the curtain never closes and the audience never leaves. If I forget my lines or fall out of character, I don't get another chance, but a bullet."

Kyle swallowed hard. He hadn't meant to give such an impassioned speech. It'd been a long time since he'd allowed himself to feel anything. He was at a loss now as to what to do with the emotions battling to escape. What was it about this woman that had such a strong hold on him? It was more than just a sexual attraction. He was at ease with her, as if he'd known her for years. Opening up felt natural, and he'd surprised himself.

"I know what it's like to be alone," Chris told him. When he looked skeptical, she smiled. "Really, I do. You can be surrounded by people, but still be alone."

"You don't seem like someone that suffers from a lack of attention," Kyle observed.

Chris laughed at the return of his welcome sarcasm. "I'm too busy with my work to have any relationships. I suppose I'm not the easiest person to get to know. I don't make it easy," she admitted.

"So we have something in common," Kyle revealed. They looked at one another for a moment, the silence between them comfortable.

"Max is the only one who knows I'm a cop," Chris said, changing the topic.

They were running out of time, and she would have to return to the downstairs room soon, as much as he'd hate to take her back. "That's good," he answered. "Keep it between the two of you, and it's best if no one else knows who I am."

"Okay," Chris agreed. "If it comes down to another tense situation, the last thing we need is for someone to slip up and give either one of us away."

"Right," Kyle said. "Jose is extremely paranoid. If he hears anything he finds suspicious, he won't stop until he gets an answer. It's safer for everyone to be in the dark on this. Well," he continued, looking at his watch. "We just need to record your ransom video for 'daddy', and then figure out how you're going to escape."

Twenty-three

Chris
Monday, 7:30 a.m.

Chris awoke to the aroma of bacon and coffee. Checking the clock on the wall, she saw she'd managed to fall back asleep for about an hour. She was surprised, given the circumstances, but she was also fully aware that everyone had their limits. No matter how much her mind was racing, her body would ultimately call the shots. Pulling all-nighters wasn't uncommon to her, and she knew she'd be okay with minimum sleep for a couple of days. Looking around, she saw that everyone else in the rec room, besides Frederick, was still asleep. Felipe and Esmeralda were gone. Chris assumed they were in the kitchen and responsible for the enticing smells.

Max had still been awake when she'd returned earlier and was concerned about her. She told him as much as possible without saying exactly who Kyle was. He seemed to accept her evasiveness, for the time being, and the simple fact that Kyle was going to help them.

Chris adjusted her legs, trying to get comfortable without being conspicuous. The easy part of their plan was recording the video, which only took a few minutes. The longer debate had been where to conceal her gun. It was now pressed firmly into her inner thigh, strapped onto it with the same belt Kyle used on his ankle. Her dress was loose and billowy, but it wasn't a small pistol. It should be okay, so long as no one searched her.

She'd spent an extra five minutes going through her cellphone and erasing anything that might indicate she was a cop. It was her personal phone, so she didn't have her professional contacts on it, but there were still a few things that would have raised questions. Now, both she and Kyle felt confident that if any of the other men were to look through it, they wouldn't be suspicious.

Kyle was asleep on the floor on the other side of the room. Carlos and Jose were upstairs. There had been a tense moment in the stairwell when they passed the two men on their way back down, but no words were exchanged.

Watching Kyle's chest rise and fall rhythmically, Chris wondered what in the hell she'd gotten herself into. The hostage situation was bad enough, but now she'd managed to get in the middle of an international arms deal.

Remembering the way she'd felt earlier when it seemed he was going to kiss her, her face grew hot, and her eyes darted away from his sleeping form. Staring into the fire instead, she compared its heat to his. With a certainty she rarely felt for anything, Chris knew if that kind of contact were ever made between them, there would be no breaking free from it. She would be lost in him. The idea of that surrender, while tempting, forced her to turn away from it.

Someone whispered her name, pulling her back from her thoughts.

Looking around, she saw it was George. Quickly crawling over to the couch, Chris knelt beside him.

"How are you feeling?" she asked him quietly.

"Not so great," he said weakly. "I can't feel my arm, Chris, and it seems like my chest is on fire."

Chris pulled his shirt open and saw immediately that the skin was red and puckered around the wound. Placing her hand lightly on his chest, she found it was hot to the touch.

"I have a fever," he told her as she examined him. His eyes had a glassy look to them, his cheeks flushed.

"Yes," Chris confirmed. "It's become infected." There weren't any red lines streaking out from it yet, but they would probably appear soon. Leaning forward, she put her lips to his forehead. He was hot, but not dangerously so. The fact that he was conscious and lucid was a good sign. "Hang in there, George," she told him, closing his shirt. "Just another twenty-four hours or so and we'll get you out of here."

George was studying her face as she spoke, and then he smiled tiredly. "You remind me of Pam," he told her.

"Pam?"

"My late wife," he answered. "She was spunky like you."

"She'd have to be to keep up with you, I think," Chris replied. She was touched by the comparison.

"You know, for the past several years, I courted death. After Pam died, I didn't have any desire to live."

"Shush," Chris hushed him. "Save your strength."

"No. I want you to hear this," he insisted. "You see, I've spent my whole life taking what the good Lord has given me for granted. I realized that a few months ago. It's taken me fifty-five years, but I finally got it. Don't let it take you that long, Chris."

Chris took his good hand in her own and wondered at the strength she found in it.

"The irony is that now, when I don't want to die, it looks like my number may be up. I've still got things to do, though," he said urgently, gripping her hand tighter. "I'm afraid if I have any say in it, Pam is going to have to wait a bit longer for our reunion."

"Of course you're not going to die," Chris confirmed. "Because I'm not going to let you." She stood to go, but he didn't let go of her hand.

"Be careful," he said hoarsely, his energy from moments before now gone.

Giving his hand one more squeeze, she went back to where Max was starting to sit up.

"How's he doing?" he asked.

"He's developed a fever, and his chest looks infected," she told him plainly. "I have to get to that boat. Tonight."

The wind still howled against the house, but the pounding on the roof seemed a little less than earlier.

"You won't be able to go out in that for a good twelve to twenty hours yet."

"That'll work," she said.

"I still don't see why you don't just wait," he complained. "Will twelve hours really make that much of a difference?"

"It could," Chris replied. "I told you before though, Max. I've got other reasons for wanting to go early. Please, just trust me."

He looked at her for a minute, weighing his options. Shrugging, he glanced over at Fredrick and then Kyle. At that moment, Jose and Carlos sauntered in, talking loudly. Apparently, the smell of cooking food woke them, too.

"I'm going to trust you know what you're doing and aren't placing us at greater risk," he said gruffly while nodding towards Jose.

"Thank you, Max." Glancing nervously at the other men, Chris shifted her legs again and arranged her dress.

"I feel responsible for these people," Max pressed. "That includes you. Let me know if I can help."

"Fair enough," Chris replied. "Right now, we need to get the first aid kit you told me about. We've got to control George's fever and see if you have any antibiotics."

"I tried, Chris. Maybe if you ask Kyle --,"

"No. Not at first, anyway. It might cause suspicion. I have a better idea." Before Max could stop her, she began to cross the room, approaching Jose.

"We need to get the first aid kit," she said bluntly.

"I already told the old fool he couldn't have it,"

Carlos growled before Jose could answer.

"It's a simple request," Chris continued, ignoring Carlos. "He'll become delirious soon," Chris explained, motioning towards George. "If you let me medicate him, he won't be a bother to you."

"If he starts moaning and groaning, I'll just throw him outside," Carlos said, angry at Chris's slight.

Jose raised his hand to silence the other man. "You may get the kit," he said quietly. "In the future though, Senorita," he cautioned, taking a deliberate step closer. "When addressing me, you will do so with respect. Comprende?"

Chris bit back the response that automatically came to mind. He reacted the way she thought he would. The request just had to be presented in a way that gave him the control and some sort of benefit. But he was a larger egomaniac than she suspected. If she weren't very careful, he would realize she wasn't afraid of him.

Looking away from his direct gaze, she nodded slowly. "Of course," she said softly. "Thank you."

Grunting, he stepped past her and motioned to Kyle, who had just stood up to watch the exchange. "Take her to get it, and then let's have some breakfast."

***

"You took a big risk, Chris," Kyle lectured.

They were standing in the upstairs hall, before an

open closet. Max said the first aid kit was there, but Chris had to dig around for it. Stopping, she looked back at Kyle and brushed some stray hair from her face.

"I had to," she explained. "George could die if we don't do anything."

"I know," Kyle replied. "But the more attention you draw to yourself, the harder it's going to be for you to get away and the greater the risk of another violent act. You should have had someone else ask."

Tilting her head slightly, Chris looked at him quizzically. Was it concern that prompted the comment or his own need to be in control? "I can take care of myself, Kyle," she finally told him. She realized even as she said it that it was a phrase she seemed to use a lot lately.

"Oh, I have no doubts about that," he said, grinning slightly. "It's just that you don't need to constantly prove it."

The truth to his statement struck a chord, causing a flush to creep into Chris's cheeks. He must have seen her anger because he quickly took her hand before she could respond, catching her off guard.

"It's okay to need someone," he said, looking at her steadily. "If you go through life doing everything on your own, that's what you'll always be, Chris. Alone."

Caught in his intense gaze, Chris couldn't turn away. She was unable to understand how this stranger could know her so well. She wanted to yell at him and tell him how wrong he was, but that would be a lie. Her biggest fear was of being alone, yet that was how she lived her life.

"Come on, Kyle; get your ass back down here!" Carlos yelled up the stairs, saving Chris from any further reflection.

Reaching over her head, Kyle took a box off the top shelf and held it out to Chris. Giving him an exasperated look, she took it.

"You knew it was there the whole time I was searching for it!"

"Like I said," he said coyly. "You need to learn to ask for help."

Brushing past him, Chris's expression conveyed her thoughts as she headed for the stairs. Trying to stifle a laugh, Kyle followed.

Twenty-four

Kyle
Monday, 2:00 p.m.

With half of the day out of the way and no further episodes of violence, Kyle was optimistic. The storm was definitely calming down, but it was still intense enough that no one in their right mind would be out in it. Of course, that didn't rule out Jose. It was almost this bad when they were caught in it the day before.

Having a couple of good meals had raised the other men's spirits. They'd even found some beer and were enjoying it while shooting a game of pool. Kyle hadn't realized Carlos was such a pool buff. But then again, he didn't make a habit of spending his free time with the man.

Kyle passed on the beer and pool. Instead, he kept to himself as usual. He was known amongst Jose's men as a loner, which was okay. He was valuable to Jose for his intelligence and contacts, not his personality. Once Kyle became submerged in his role, he found the only way to preserve himself was to withdraw. He dulled his emotions and closed the doors on his innermost feelings, placing a buffer between what he felt and what he was doing. That's what cost him his marriage early on, before he'd even left for Mexico. The irony of the advice he gave to Chris wasn't lost on him.

He tried to convince his wife that he was still the same person, if she could just wait for him to finish the assignment. But apparently their bond wasn't strong enough, and she was either unwilling or unable to understand.

Now, as Kyle studied all the occupants in the room, he wondered if he really knew who he was anymore. The lines had blurred, and he no longer remembered how it was to feel in a normal way. His eyes settled on Chris, and there was a stirring within him. For some reason, this woman was able to reach a part of him he'd forgotten about.

Loud laughter erupted from the men at the pool table, putting Kyle on guard. Shifting slightly, he watched carefully as Carlos and Felipe engaged in some friendly banter. Relaxed was one thing, but them getting drunk was an extra risk he didn't want to have to deal with.

"You didn't call the pocket," Felipe exclaimed.

"You calling me a liar?"

Felipe stared at Carlos for a solid minute before a smile slowly spread across his face. "Of course not! I must not have heard you."

"Perhaps we need a witness," Carlos pressed, unwilling to let it go. "Karen!" he bellowed. "Come over here and watch us play. You can be my good luck charm."

Kyle saw the small Ecuadorian woman stand up hesitantly from where she'd been sitting with Cathy. Glancing furtively at her husband, she wrung her hands together before taking a timid step towards them.

Rico jumped up from the chess table and went to stand in front of his wife. "Sit down," he instructed, pointing back at the couch. When she paused, staring past him fearfully at the other men, he put an arm gently around her shoulders to help guide her. "Sit down, Karen. You don't have to do anything."

Kyle pushed away from the wall and resisted the urge to look at Chris. He was certain she would also be positioning herself to act if they had to.

Carlos slowly set his beer down and motioned for Rico to approach him. "You want in on this game, mi hermano?"

"I am not your brother," Rico spat. Stopping short of the table, the much smaller man looked up at Carlos with contempt. "You do not represent me or my people."

With lightning speed, Carlos lunged forward and swung his pool cue around, connecting solidly with the side of Rico's head. His legs buckled and he slid to the floor, unconscious.

Kyle was already across the room, gun in hand; but to his surprise, Carlos broke out laughing and stepped away from the fallen man.

"Our friend has a glass jaw," he told Felipe. "Too bad, Karen!" he shouted again when the young woman moved to her husband's side. "I have a *very* strong jaw."

"Leave them alone," Jose intervened. "Finish the game and take a nap. I don't need drunken fools right now."

Rico was already groaning and trying to sit up. Holding the side of his head, he kept asking Karen what happened.

"Come on," Kyle offered, lifting the man to his feet. Rico tried to shrug off his help but found he needed the extra arm to keep him up. Since both of the couches were occupied, Kyle led him to one of the two recliners. "Take care of him," he told Karen. When she looked at him with wide, frightened eyes, he lowered his voice. "Keep him quiet."

Glancing towards Chris, he saw she was on her feet. He gave one firm shake of his head. Thankfully, she understood and went back to tending to George's shoulder. If they were going to get through the rest of the day and carry out their plan, they'd have to run some interference. One more outburst like this and things were going to go from bad to much, much worse.

Twenty-five

Chris
Monday, 2:30 P.M.

Chris finished applying the fresh dressing to George's shoulder and looked up to find Kyle still watching her. His face was neutral, but his eyes locked onto her with what felt like a physical connection.

Chris quickly looked away before anyone noticed the exchange. She realized her pulse was racing and struggled to slow her breathing. Looking for a distraction, she went about taking George's temperature and forgot everything else when she saw the results. Dorothy came over as she was digging through the first aid kit for the Tylenol.

"How's he doing?" she asked while placing one of her own hands against his clammy forehead.

"Not so well," Chris replied. Smiling, she held the bottle up that she'd successfully found but then frowned again. "I don't think he can swallow pills anymore," she explained. "I'm going to have to crush them. Hand me that glass, would you?"

Dorothy got the glass from the end table and sat next to Chris, watching as the other woman went about the task. She kept expecting to wake up from her nightmare, but it wasn't happening. What had been her safe haven for so many years was now a prison, and she was helpless to do anything about it.

"I'm very worried about Cathy," Dorothy said as Chris tried to get George to drink the mixture. "She's completely unresponsive, and I can't get her to eat or drink anything. She just sits there staring and shaking. I don't even think she's slept."

"She's in shock," Chris explained, although she knew Dorothy had already figured that out. "She'll be okay without the food, but you need to get her to drink. Force her if you have to. Get Karen to help. Keep her warm. There really isn't anything else we can do for now."

"The poor woman," Dorothy continued. "She and Desmond were married just two months ago. They waited until now to take a honeymoon because of Desmond's duties."

"Chris!"

Looking up at her urgently whispered name, Chris saw that Max was kneeling next to the chair Rico was sprawled out in. While the young man was holding a hand to his head, he appeared alert. Max waved at her, beckoning her to join them.

Feeling pulled in way too many directions, Chris gritted her teeth and handed the medicated water to Dorothy. "Here," she instructed. "Do your best to get George to drink the rest of this. The infection is getting worse, and I'm afraid his fever will be out of control soon if we can't manage it. There weren't any antibiotics in the bag. Can you think of anywhere else you might have some?"

Shaking her head, Dorothy took the water. "No. I'm sorry, Chris. I already checked the bathroom medicine cabinets."

Resisting the urge to sigh, she instead forced an encouraging smile for the older woman before joining Max, Karen, and Rico. Karen was holding her husband's hand and looking extremely worried.

"I'm afraid he has a concussion," Max stated without preamble. "Should we try to keep him awake or something?"

Crouching down in front of the recliner, Chris looked up into Rico's slightly pale face. "Do you know who and where you are?" When Rico nodded, she leaned forward and pulled his hand away from his face so she could see the wound. It wasn't bleeding, but there was a nice lump next to his left eyebrow and some bruising around his eye. Cupping her hand over first one eye and then the next, she checked his pupils for a normal reaction.

"Feel like you're going to throw up?"

Shaking his head slightly, the movement caused him to wince. "No, but I have a headache."

"I'll bet you do," Chris replied. "You got hit upside the head with a pool stick. Any dizziness?"

"No. I'm fine," he urged, looking at Karen.

"I'm sure you are," Chris agreed. "Probably just a

mild concussion. Here," she continued, pulling the Tylenol out of her pocket. "Take one of these. If it helps the headache then you probably don't have anything to worry about. You don't have any serious signs or symptoms, but we'll need to keep an eye on you."

"How do you know so much?" Karen asked. She looked relieved and finally sat down in the chair next to her husband.

"I do a lot of hiking," Chris told her while shifting her focus to the young woman. "So I've taken several first aid and outdoor survival courses." While all of that was true, she'd learned most of her trauma first aid through her police training. "I'm actually more concerned about *you*," she continued, pointing a finger at Karen. "I noticed you've been holding your stomach more today."

Glancing furtively at first Rico and then Chris, Karen took a deep, shuddering breath. "I've had some cramping."

"What?" Rico almost shouted, coming partway out of his chair.

"That is exactly what she doesn't need!" Chris chastised. Turning on Rico, she continued her lecture in hushed tones. "I know you just want to protect Karen, but confronting these men and going out of your way to antagonize them is only making this worse for her. If you really want to help her, you'll have to put your ego aside, Rico."

Glancing at his wife, Rico could see she was near tears. Looking guilty, he reached out and took her hand back into his own. "I'm sorry," he whispered. "Do you think the baby is okay?"

Nodding, Karen squeezed his hand. "Esmerelda said it's probably some Braxton Hicks contractions. It's false labor," she rushed to explain when Rico paled even further. "Totally harmless. Esmerelda said she had it with all of her kids. She's flooding me with water and told me to keep off my feet since stress and dehydration can make them worse."

The information hardened Chris's resolve to get to the boat. It also sharpened her anger over the completely senseless situation. A life was taken and all of them plunged into a nightmare without a moments regret. In fact, Carlos seemed to be enjoying himself. The clacking of the pool balls was driving her crazy, but she figured it was at least keeping him occupied so his attention was on something else other than them.

Dorothy joined them, handing Chris the empty glass. "He drank it all."

"Great. Thank you, Dorothy. It's going to be okay," she added. Looking around at them all, she dropped her voice to a whisper "They'll be gone in the morning, and I have a plan to get us some help sooner than Friday. Just keep to yourselves," she urged, looking pointedly at Rico.

The hostages spent the rest of the day being as inconspicuous as possible. Dorothy kept constant vigil over Cathy while Max and Chris tended to George. Rico slept most of the time, to Chris's relief, leaving Karen and Esmeralda to talk quietly while Ken and David kept to themselves. At the moment, they were involved in what was likely the one hundredth game of chess. It seemed to have a calming effect on both of them.

***

David slouched further in his seat as he stared at the board. After looking fleetingly at the Guerillas scattered around the room, he studied the chess pieces again. This had been his routine for the past several hours. His father never complained about the time he took to complete a move.

He was certain that at any minute someone would be shot again without warning. He had no intention of being caught off guard this time. When Desmond was killed, it all seemed so surreal. One minute he was standing there talking, the next he was dead on the floor.

David had never seen a dead person before, and he hoped to never see one again.

The special effects in movies are more realistic, he thought. The man who'd been talking with him earlier about the Marines couldn't be lying cold and stiff now out in the rain.

His chest getting tighter and the cold knot of fear in his stomach starting to radiate out, David looked once again at the armed men. Reassured that nothing had changed, his breathing slowed again. The cold sweat on his palms dried as he rubbed them on his jeans.

"David," Ken said quietly.

Jumping, David looked at his father. His eyes

resembled those of a rabbit caught in a snare.

"Take a deep breath, David," Ken whispered soothingly. He recognized the panic attacks for what they were, and he was afraid David would lose control, drawing unwanted attention to himself. "It's okay, son," he continued, patting the boy's knee under the small table. "Things are under control now. They're going to leave in the morning, and this will all be over. I won't let anything bad happen to you."

David looked at his father and tried to concentrate on what he was saying. He found that when he listened to his dad talk, he forgot what was happening for the moment and the cold edge of fear subsided.

Funny, how he suddenly found himself relying on his father. Just a couple of weeks ago, he swore he would never talk to the man again. His life changed dramatically earlier that year, and he placed all of the blame on Ken. His father's affair ripped the family apart, and all the counseling in the world wouldn't change that.

Then, there was his job. It always seemed to come first. David detested computers because of it. His father had never really been there for him. Since the breakup, Ken steadily attempted to establish a relationship with him. Claiming his unhappiness had clouded things, he professed that now he was able to be the father he should have always been.

That was what his dad was trying to get him to believe, anyway. This trip was his idea to finally bring them together, but David had dug his heals in, determined to prove to his father that he was wasting his time. He certainly didn't think he needed him or wanted him. He didn't think he needed anyone.

As Ken continued to talk, David focused even harder on the words, desperately trying to find an anchor in the storm of emotions raging within him. Reaching out absently, he grasped the hand at his knee. His father was the one real thing in all of this madness. If he could just hold on to him, it would be all right. When his dad squeezed his hand, David squeezed back.

They would make it through this together.

Twenty-six

Chris
Monday, 7:00 P.M

Sitting around the large dining table, the scene was surreal to Chris. Breakfast and lunch were served in shifts, brought into the recreation room on trays. For some reason, Jose decided to congregate in the dining hall that evening.

Esmerelda made her usual full-course meal. The only people enjoying it, however, were the four guerrillas. Kyle offered to stay in the other room to watch over Cathy and the two sleeping forms of George and Rico. Since he didn't throw up and the headache eased up with the Tylenol, Chris told Rico to go ahead and rest.

Seated in the handsome room, observing the other guests pick uneasily at their food, Chris felt like Alice at the Mad Hatter's tea party. Jose and Carlos were laughing loudly over some raunchy joke. Felipe and Fredrick grinned while they greedily consumed their food. If it weren't for the handguns placed carefully next to their plates, they might pass as a regular group of vacationers.

Chris looked at the chicken casserole, trying to force herself to eat. She knew that while sleep wasn't essential for another day or two, food was. If she was going to keep her stamina up, she'd have to eat. Taking a bite, Chris thought over her plans. The trek through the jungle wouldn't be easy, especially with the torrential downpour assaulting the island. The streams she crossed earlier on her hike would now be hard to navigate. Her experience with boating was limited, so it would take her a while to get coordinated once she headed out onto open water.

The laughter stopped. Chris looked up to find Jose watching her intensely. Shifting in her seat, she had the uncanny feeling he had somehow read her mind. She met his gaze just long enough to acknowledge him and then continued eating.

"Are you enjoying your dinner, Senorita?" he asked her politely, in stark contrast to his piercing glare.

Remembering his warning from earlier in the day, Chris chose her words carefully. "It's very good," she replied evenly, putting her fork down and raising her eyes to meet his scrutiny once again. "Thank you for sharing it with us."

Tilting his chin slightly, Jose seemed to consider whether or not she was mocking him. Slowly smiling, he gestured towards her with his wineglass. "You are a fast learner," he said, taking a long sip of the amber liquid. "That is good."

Turning to Esmerelda, he set the glass down and clapped his hands loudly, nearly causing David to fall out of his chair. "We will have dessert!" he shouted.

Taking another long swallow of beer, Carlos slammed the empty bottle down next to two others in front of him.

He'd followed his leader's advice and taken a long nap earlier. Having him out of the room was a huge relief to Chris, and she noticed Felipe and Fredrick weren't as obnoxious when he wasn't around. Jose remained a mystery. His aloofness and arrogance were misleading, and she was beginning to think he was much smarter than he let on.

Popping the top off another bottle from what seemed an endless supply of beer, Carlos continued to get louder. "I hope it's chocolate cake," he barked at the cook's back as she hurried past him. Reaching out, he slapped her on her plump rear, laughing at her gasp of surprise.

Chris expected to see the white rabbit run through anytime now.

Twenty-seven

Kyle
Monday, 7:30 P.M.

Kyle watched without comment as everyone filed back into the room, taking the plate of food Karen offered him. Carlos was half-drunk again and grumbling loudly about the dessert. Apparently, he was disappointed they were served apple crisp.

These next few hours might prove the most dangerous. At least Rico was still sleeping, so he wouldn't be at risk of pissing Carlos off again. Kyle knew from extensive experience that when drunk, the unruly man could be either overly friendly or itching for a fight. It was at times like this that Jose's lack of management drove him crazy. It was a miracle they all hadn't been either killed or arrested in just the past year alone.

Dorothy made a beeline for Cathy. She was holding what Kyle suspected was some sort of broth. He'd heard her asking Esmerelda to make it earlier. The older woman sat down next to her prone form on the couch and coaxed her to sit up. Holding the bowl to her mouth, she tipped it while whispering to her. Cathy's only form of acknowledgment was to blink and flinch away from the liquid, causing some of it to spill down her chin and onto the front of her shirt.

Carlos immediately went back to the pool table, racking the balls. Grabbing a pool stick, he sauntered over to where Chris and Max were hovering over George.

"Chris!" he spat loudly.

Kyle's pulse quickened, and he forced himself not to intervene unless it became absolutely necessary.

Choosing not to answer, Chris simply looked up at him disdainfully.

"Come play with me, babe. That is, if your keeper will permit it," he added, sneering over at Kyle.

Kyle simply shrugged and looked away, feigning disinterest. This was the situation they'd hoped to avoid. So long as Carlos got what he wanted, it would be all right. But the moment he felt challenged, all hell would break loose.

Following Kyle's lead, Chris got to her feet and, facing Carlos, snatched the pool stick from his hand. At his surprised look, she brushed past him and proceeded to break the balls. By the fourth round of play, Chris cleared the table. Winking at Carlos, she sank the eight ball in the pocket she'd called.

"Now, if you don't mind," she said politely to him as she handed the stick back. "I would like to get some sleep."

Looking her over slowly, his glazed eyes eventually

came to rest on her face. "Perhaps I want to play *another* game," he challenged, not showing any intention of getting out of her way.

"If you want to get your ass kicked again, then fine. Rack 'em up."

Laughing loudly, Carlos stepped aside, letting her pass. "If I had to get my ass kicked by anyone, Senorita," he said to her back. "I'd call you anytime."

Kyle feared a bad reaction from Carlos at being beaten so badly, but once again, Chris's intuition to the men's personalities proved correct. Carlos was amused rather than angered at it, and it actually eased the tension between the two to a degree.

They had less than ten hours to go. Ten hours until the men would be on the boat arriving early the next morning. His goal was to make sure all of the people in that room were still alive when that happened. There might even be a chance that he could end this mess with Chang's arrest.

Glancing at his watch, Kyle then slipped out of the rec room and went to the front door of the estate. Pulling it open, he looked out into the shadowed landscape that was further obscured by the driven rain. The wind was still howling but not nearly as fiercely as before.

Moving up next to him in the semi-darkness, Jose lit a cigar he'd taken from the den. Blowing the smoke out into the night, he spoke without turning to face Kyle. "By morning, we'll finally be gone from this place," he said, his voice a deep baritone that somehow resonated over the howl of the storm without effort. "Those weapons are an essential part of our fight, Kyle. I will be counting on you tomorrow. Do not let me down."

Retreating from the entrance without another word, Jose went back down the hall, leaving a thin trail of smoke behind him.

Alone again, Kyle closed his eyes and let the wind creeping under the patio eaves cool his face. As always, Jose spoke with subtle innuendoes and hidden threats. He was letting Kyle know that, although he trusted him enough to have him working by his side, he still didn't understand him and to that end, was watching. Always watching … and waiting. Breathing deeply, Kyle looked again into the shadows upon shadows and was reminded of the many layers of himself. The layer Jose saw, that Chris saw, and that he himself was looking for but couldn't find. Was it still there among the darkness? The whispering of his innermost thoughts was becoming lost in the haze and the harder he tried to listen … the more it faded away.

Twenty-eight

Chris
Tuesday, 12:30 A.M.

Chris opened her eyes and looked to where Kyle and Fredrick were sitting in their usual spots. She hadn't actually been asleep. For the first three hours, while Carlos and Felipe were standing watch, she dozed on and off. Carlos was so drunk by then that he wasn't a concern as he could hardly stand up. Since Kyle had replaced him a half hour ago, she'd been wide awake.

Forcing herself to wait was the hardest part. It was still a little early, but this three-hour stretch during Kyle's shift was the only shot they had. If she made it to the boat before sunrise, which should be around 5:30, she'd simply hide and then leave at five.

Max said it would normally take two hours to get to the mainland, but it would likely be closer to three. While the worst of the storm was hours behind them, the water would still be rough. With the schedule Kyle laid out for the exchange, she should be able to reach his contacts in time to get the coordinates to them. But *only* if she made it off the island before they did.

It was tempting to scratch the whole idea and just huddle there on the floor until they left. Let Kyle fend for himself the way he had been for the past two years. But the cop in her wouldn't allow it. She was going to make them *pay* for what they did to Desmond. Chris was trusting Kyle to keep Jose and his men from hurting anyone else.

George moaned weakly on the couch beside her, his fever now beyond the reach of the limited medicine they had. Red streaks of infection, mapping the invasion into his bloodstream, had shown up on his chest late that evening. There wasn't much time left before it would be too late for any sort of intervention.

Moving up next to him, Chris placed her hand on his hot forehead and kissed him softly on the cheek. His eyelids fluttered but didn't open. "Hold on, George," she whispered to him, pressing her face to his. "I'm going to get you out of here. I promise."

"I know, Pam," he moaned, mistaking her for his late wife in his delirium. "We'll take a trip to the States next year, as soon as I'm retired." The effort to speak seemed too much for him, and he slipped back into a feverish sleep.

With renewed determination, Chris stood and quietly picked her way around the sleeping forms of her friends. Max silently watched her go, the only other person awake. Their eyes met as she stepped around him and with a curt nod, he relayed his support.

"What the hell do you want?" Kyle snapped as she approached the men.

"I need to use the bathroom," Chris said through gritted teeth.

"You can wait until morning," Kyle said, dismissing her.

"Do you think," she continued with mock anger, "that I would be here asking you if it were at all possible for me to wait?"

"I'll take her," Fredrick offered, grinning.

"No," Kyle ordered, grabbing Chris by the upper arm. "If she wants some time alone with me, I'll give it to her."

Fredrick snickered in response. "Don't be too long. Jose will be down to check on us in a couple hours."

Kyle pulled her out into the foyer, and Chris made of a show of struggling to free herself from his grasp. Taking both of her arms, he pushed her in front of him as Fredrick watched with amusement.

***

The dim bathroom light spilled out into the short hallway where Kyle stood. The downstairs restroom was at the back of the house, tucked away between the sunroom and kitchen. It would allow both privacy and easy access for Chris to the backdoor.

Chris was silhouetted in the doorway, a ceramic soap

dispenser gripped at her side.

"Come on, Chris, hit me!" Kyle demanded, turning his head toward her when she didn't move. "We don't have much time. Just do it hard enough to leave a good mark, right about here," he directed, indicating a spot over his right eyebrow.

Now that the time had come, Chris's resolve was threatening to waver. Her heart was racing, the pressure building behind her temples. Squeezing her eyes against the throbbing, Chris took a deep breath and opening them, swung out at Kyle's forehead. The impact was harder than she intended, creating a sickening sound similar to a bat hitting a baseball. Grimacing, she watched Kyle as he silently held his face in his hands for a full minute before finally lowering them and grinning a her.

"Shit, Chris!" he exclaimed. "I said hard enough to leave a mark, not a dent!" Wiping at the blood that was starting to flow into his eye, he smiled at the look on her face. "I'm okay," he assured her, taking the dispenser out of her hand and placing it on the floor near where he would lay. "It'll just make it more convincing."

"I'm sorry, Kyle," she finally said, fighting the urge to tend to the cut she'd created. "I guess I'm not used to hitting men in the head with blunt objects."

"Yeah, only your fists and knees," he mocked. "Come on," he pressed, pulling her out into the hallway. "I'll stall for as long as I can."

"I know you will," she replied, looking up into his grey eyes that always seemed to be changing. Now, they were full of concern and a hint of something else she couldn't quite discern.

"Be careful, Chris."

Standing there in the space so small that they were nearly touching, Chris could feel the heat from his body and smell the musky scent she'd become familiar with. But as the tension grew between them, she recognized the other element in his features. It was fear. Not for himself, but for her.

Chris had never wanted or needed anyone else to worry about her. She was used to taking care of herself. Of making sure no one else had the burden of her emotional needs. To allow closeness meant you cared, and it would only lead to heartache. She suddenly realized that she'd learned that lesson several times over at a very young age. It took her standing there, in the dimly lit hallway with a man she hardly knew, to come to this understanding. A man that was looking at her in a way that would usually make her run away, but instead it pulled her closer to that ledge she was so terrified of falling over.

Kyle must have seen the longing in her, because he closed the space between them. His hands pressed into her back, forcing their bodies together, and causing a small sigh to escape her lips. Encouraged by the sound, his embrace tightened until she could feel the hard outlines of the muscles of his chest. She desperately wanted to reach under his shirt to explore them. Instead, she ran her hands up his biceps and buried her fingers in his tangle of hair, pulling him down towards her.

His breath was hot on her face, and then his lips

found hers with a hunger that shocked her. Any rational thought was instantly replaced with a desire to be lost in that passion, and Chris responded fervently, already consumed by it.

In a motion that was almost violent, Kyle slid his hands onto her upper arms and forced them apart.

Gasping for air, Chris blinked furiously, trying to clear her head. *What were they doing?* Stumbling back a step, she was acutely aware of every spot where their bodies had connected due to the burning sensation left in its wake.

Taking a deep breath, Kyle ran his hands over his face, wincing when he touched the rising lump on his temple. "You should go," he urged, his voice hoarse.

But Chris had already started down the hall and didn't look back.

Twenty-nine

Chris
Tuesday, 1:00 A.M.

The darkness around Chris was complete, and she struggled to find the trail that led back to her cabin. She made it out the back door and into the gardens undetected, but it was difficult to get her bearings with the storm crashing around her. On top of that, this was an unfamiliar part of the yard. Finally, she found a way through the vegetation and around the side of the house. She could just make out the trailhead in the weak light from the porch.

She reluctantly agreed with Kyle that giving her one of the flashlights would be too risky. He wouldn't have taken it with them to go to the bathroom. There were only a couple between them all, and the second one was upstairs with Jose. There was one in her cabin. She had to go there anyway to get her laptop and change into something she could hike in.

Chris looked back once at the shuttered windows

and, sending up a final prayer, skirted the edge of the dim light. As she walked again into the darkness of the trail, tripping over fallen branches and fronds, she found herself in a world of shadows. The storm brought the jungle around her to life, and it reached out as if to pull her in.

It's just my imagination, she thought as invisible hands caressed her bare arms in the darkness. What seemed an eternity was, in reality, only minutes before the shadows lightened and the sand stung her eyes as she emerged onto the beach.

The wind was considerably lighter since Kyle's visit the night before, but it still had enough fury to hurl the sand at the cabin and anything else senseless enough to be exposed.

With an arm over her eyes in a weak attempt to protect them, Chris stumbled up the stairs and finally took refuge in the dark cabin. Before the door had even blown shut, she was in the kitchen rummaging through the cupboards for the flashlight she knew was there. She didn't remember seeing any power lines and figured the cables leading to the building must be buried, but she didn't even try the light switch. As unlikely as it was that anyone was outside or looking for her, she couldn't take the chance of turning the place into a beacon.

Feeling blindly around the shelves, she found the light along with some candles and matches. With a whimper of relief, she turned it on, pushing back the darkness that nearly suffocated her.

Sliding down to the floor, Chris sat the flashlight

upright between her legs and took slow, deep breaths.

Get a grip, Chris, she ordered herself.

Feeling instantly guilty for having wasted several precious minutes, she jumped to her feet and went quickly to the bedroom. Stripping off the soaked sundress, she thankfully unstrapped the gun from her thigh, not bothering to even look at the damage the belt left behind. Slipping into a pair of jeans and a sweatshirt, she hesitated for only a moment before removing her shoulder holster from the suitcase. Strapping it into place under the loose-fitting top, she figured it was the best way to carry it. If all went well, she wouldn't be at risk of being searched again. It gave her a solid, reassuring feeling.

Grabbing a towel from the bathroom, she wrapped it around the small laptop before stuffing it inside her backpack, the one carryon she brought. She used it for her day hikes and it was supposed to be waterproof, but she wasn't taking any chances. A couple of granola bars, a bottle of water, and a dry shirt to change into took up the rest of the space. She strapped it on, snug against her back.

Back outside, it took a frustrating fifteen minutes to locate the trail Karen had led her on the day before. Once on it though, Chris plunged ahead recklessly, her flashlight playing over the jungle floor in crazy patterns.

According to Max, she needed to follow this across the island and to the fork she distinctly remembered. There was a small wooden sign that simply said 'West Cove'. When she'd asked Karen about it, her guide said it was just a small bay and not worth the time to go explore. If the weather didn't hold her up too much, she should be able to get there in less than two hours. Just enough time to get the boat situated and headed in the right direction before sunup.

But the going was treacherous. The ground was a literal bog in places as the incredible amount of water suddenly unleased had nowhere else to go. The first stream she crossed pushed savagely at her knees, when only two days before it had barely brushed her ankles. Knowing of at least two larger ones to come, Chris worried that maybe she *wouldn't* be able to reach the boat to bring help in time for Kyle.

Kyle … he was a mystery to her that she badly wanted to solve. Perhaps she was so intrigued by him because he somehow forced her to look inside herself for the answers to his riddle. Behind the mask was a very complex person, and in a sense, she wore a mask of her own. It wasn't as obvious as his, but it was there. Hers was more of a blockade to the emotions that she was afraid to open herself up to.

If people thought she was as strong as she made herself out to be, believed she really didn't need or want their help, then they wouldn't assert themselves. She had friends, sure, but in order to let a relationship evolve to the next, deeper level, there had to be an exchange of trust.

I'm afraid to let anyone in, Chris realized as she strained to stay on the trail.

Out there, alone in the storm-tossed jungle, she was

confronted with her greatest fear. It wasn't the group of terrorist's, armed and eager for glory, or of being lost in the dark, or at sea in the small boat. It was the giving of herself to another person, of trusting someone enough to let him or her in … to need them.

The therapist she'd been forced to see when she was sixteen, after her kidnapping, would have said this was a direct result of her forced imprisonment. But Chris knew there were more layers to it than that. Most of the memories of the two weeks she'd spent in the dark basement were locked away deep inside. She only recalled small snippets of conversations and fleeting images that randomly surfaced during nightmares. Her current psychological state was born more from the betrayal she experienced afterwards by the people who were supposed to always be there, no matter what. A rash of failed relationships further defined this in her early twenties.

By keeping her emotions to herself, Chris thought this prevented her from being hurt. Because she knew that love *did* hurt, much worse than a bullet wound.

I'm not a child anymore, Chris thought angrily. *I can't go through my life afraid of giving another person my love. I'm not nearly as brave as everyone thinks I am. I'm a coward.*

Stopping before a fallen tree, Chris leaned into it and rested her forehead against the cool bark. The warm rain mingled with her tears as she finally let go and allowed herself to admit to the pain of her self-imprisoned loneliness. She didn't want to be alone. To experience life through only her eyes.

Wiping briskly at her face, Chris took a deep breath

to steady herself and fought the urge to acknowledge that her boss, Mick, was right. Apparently, all she needed was to go on vacation, be held hostage by a band of guerrillas, and get lost in a hurricane to find herself. Grinning now, she shined the light over the collapsed log and decided to climb over it.

Although her situation was grim, Chris had a new sense of direction. She vowed to follow through and make some changes. Things were going to be different now.

Dropping down over the other side of the tree, her optimism turned to dread when, instead of landing on solid ground, she found herself sliding down a deep, muddy crevasse.

Thirty

Kyle
Tuesday, 2:00 A.M.

Kyle feigned unconsciousness as Carlos kicked at him again, then finally groaned and rolled to his side. "What the hell happened?" he demanded groggily while putting a hand to his temple. When he brought it away and saw the blood, he swore louder and sat up.

"Where is she?" Carlos snapped, not offering a hand.

Kyle looked beyond Carlos and saw that Fredrick stood nervously behind the larger man. It had been nearly an hour since Chris left, and Kyle was guessing Fredrick must have gone and woken Carlos to check on things when they didn't return.

"Last thing I remember is her walking into the bathroom," Kyle explained as he staggered to his feet. "She must have hit me with something."

Carlos bent over to pick up the soap dispenser, tossing it a couple of times in his hand before snickering at Kyle. "I knew you'd need some help with that wildcat," he scoffed. "Now there's gonna be hell to pay."

"Am I leading a bunch of idiots?" Jose suddenly bellowed, appearing in the sunroom at the end of the short hall. "I found Felipe out there by himself, half asleep, and it's taken the three of you to determine that the woman somehow *escaped*?"

Fredrick quickly back peddled past Jose, keeping his head down. "I'll … um, go back to rec room."

Kyle turned to face the fuming rebel, making sure he saw the blood on his head, and tried to get control of the situation. This was a critical moment which could dictate who would live and die.

"I take full responsibility, Jose," he said sheepishly. "I let my guard down and she surprised me."

"Did she have help?" he pressed. "Is anyone else missing?"

"No," Kyle said without hesitating. "It was just her. I still have her phone, though," he added as an afterthought, pulling it from his back pocket. "I'm ready to send it to her father as soon as we're clear of the exchange later today."

"Of all my people," Jose replied quietly, ignoring Kyle's attempt to give things a positive spin. "You are the last one I'd expect to make such an error." Staring intently at Kyle, his eyes narrowed. "What the hell were you thinking? Why would you ever take her off on your own and then turn your back?" His voice was steadily rising as he crossed the short space between them, walking closer to Kyle. "I am disappointed, Amigo," he continued, his voice dropping again. "I demand more from you."

Kyle breathed a sigh of relief when it appeared that his rage was in check. It would likely mean he'd never become Jose's top lieutenant, but given the fact that he hoped to put the man behind bars before the end of the day, that hardly mattered. In order to be convincing, however, Kyle had to make him believe that it did.

Remembering to never break eye contact, he looked earnestly at Jose and gripped the other man by the shoulders. "I'm sorry. I failed you. I give you my word that it won't happen again. I'll do everything I can to meet your expectations, Jose, and to help you bring your people the supplies they need to fight the war."

The patriotic words seemed to soften what was left of the leader's anger, and he returned the mock embrace. But then he turned to Carlos with his next order. "You will go after the girl," he told him. "We will make an example of her for her friends."

"There's nothing I'd like to do more than to teach that bitch a lesson," Carlos replied. "But the boat will be here in, what, four or five hours? She could be literally anywhere on this freaking island. I say let her be cold and miserable by herself. She's not worth the effort."

For the first time ever, Kyle liked Carlos an awful lot. Jose, on the other hand, was not biting. He was shaking his head, and Kyle could see the same single-mindedness that had forced them out into the storm earlier. Chris was a loose string Jose would not allow, and he intended to cut it off, no matter how senseless chasing her was.

"No," Jose ordered. "She will be found and brought

back. This is not a large island. She could be in her cabin right now, possibly using a device that was overlooked!"

"I'll go," Kyle volunteered. When all eyes turned to him, he focused on Jose. "It's my mess, and I should clean it up. My shift is just ending, so it'll be on my own time. I'll find her," he continued. "I promise you."

Jose contemplated the situation only briefly before slapping Kyle on the back. "Go now," he said loudly. "But pay attention to the time. Be sure you're back before seven. If you find her and she slows you down, shoot her."

***

3:00 A.M.

Kyle had made his way quickly to the cabin just to make sure Chris wasn't still there. As expected, he found it empty. Concentrating on the edge of the jungle near where he knew the trail was, he spent nearly half an hour before finding it. If it weren't for the impressions Chris left in the soft mud, it would have taken much longer.

As he headed into the thick foliage, Kyle was thankful that the storm was loosening its grip on the island a little more each hour. But it was still enough to prevent any attempt on the water in a small boat. He hoped it would continue to quickly pass over them. He briefly debated whether he should just sit in her cabin for a couple of hours before going back and claiming defeat. But after seeing the condition of the jungle, he had a sense of urgency to find Chris and make sure she got off in the boat safely. Picking his way carefully over fallen branches and other debris, he questioned the whole plan again. He understood why Chris wanted to attempt it, but it was beginning to feel like it wasn't worth the risk.

While thinking about Chris, Kyle found the iron band that normally gripped his emotions continued to loosen. It was as if he was seeing himself through someone else's eyes. And he could glimpse the exposed remnants that were in there somewhere. With her, he could face the fear of looking and possibly not finding anything.

Shaking his head, he contemplated the situation. He hardly knew her, but he felt as if he'd been reunited with a long-lost friend. He'd never believed in such things before. Perhaps it was the intensity of how they met that created it, but there was something there he couldn't deny. That he couldn't let *her* deny.

"Of course, that's if we both survive this," he said aloud.

He came up to a large, fallen tree and was about to leap over it when he heard his name being desperately called.

"Kyle!" Chris yelled from bellow. "Is that you? Kyle! I'm down here. Don't go over the log!"

Leaning against the trunk, Kyle shined his flashlight over the other side and found the ground was washed away beyond it. Several feet down a steep embankment, Chris sat crouched on a small ledge, holding on precariously to some roots sticking out of the mud above her. Water raged below, swift enough to look dangerous.

"Hold on, Chris!" Kyle yelled back.

As Chris squinted up into his light, she let out a shriek of terror when the ground under her suddenly disappeared.

Thirty-one

Chris
Tuesday, 3:30 A.M.

Chris sent up a silent prayer of thanks for the extra days she'd spent in the gym, as she held onto the exposed roots with all of her strength. Her feet dangled over a dark pit where the ground had been, and she could just make out the dark, churning water about 20 feet below.

Kyle's flashlight bobbed wildly above her, and she tried to focus on it. She didn't know how much longer she could hold on. Finally, the light steadied and shined down on her as Kyle reappeared. Leaning over the log, he was holding what looked like his belt.

"See if you can reach this, Chris!" Straddling the tree trunk, Kyle balanced precariously on its slippery surface while stretching as far as he could.

Kicking out at the remnants of the muddy cliffside, Chris found some purchase and, taking a deep breath, made a frantic lunge for the belt. Her right hand closed around it but almost immediately began slipping down its length. Just when she was about to fall, Kyle took hold of her wrist in a firm grip.

Gasping, she flailed with her other hand until he caught that one, too, and together they struggled in the rain and mud. After what felt like an eternity, she finally fell in a heap on top of him on the far side of the log.

Breathing heavily, Chris sat for several minutes, letting the rain wash the mud away and trying to catch her breath. She was soaked through and had gotten chilled while sitting immobile for so long.

Kyle must have seen that she was shaking because he wrapped his arms around her, pulling her to him. "Are you okay?"

When she nodded silently, he continued talking, his voice muffled by her hair. "Jose nearly had a fit when he found out you were gone, but I think he's under control now. He wanted to send Carlos out to find you, but Carlos wasn't too happy with the idea. Because of that, I was able to volunteer without seeming suspicious."

Chris was finding it hard to concentrate now on what he was saying, with his arms around her and being pressed up against his warm body. "Oh, well," she stammered. "That's good. I guess. But what will they say when you return without me?"

"Jose can hardly wait any longer than seven thirty, when we have to leave in order to meet the other boat in time. I'll tell him I found you, but you put up a fight so I had to shoot you. There won't be time to confirm it, and I'm hoping it will placate his need for whatever lesson he feels is justified for the rest of the hostages. It might help us get off of this damn rock without anyone else being killed. I hope."

Nodding, Chris snuggled in a little further. "Hopefully the boat is still intact."

Reluctantly, Kyle got to his feet and shined the light on his watch. "It's nearly four now," he explained. "If I'm not back before seven, Jose will probably send one of the guys looking for me, so I'll make it six thirty or so. We better hurry and find that boat. How much further do you think it is from here?"

"If I remember correctly, it's less than half an hour from here, but we'll have to find somewhere that we can cross this mess. That landslide used to be where the trail led down to the water. So long as we don't have to go too far to get around it, you should have plenty of time to get back."

Pulling Chris to her feet, Kyle led the way upstream, and it didn't take long to find a lower spot with some large rocks that made the crossing easier. Chris was relieved to see the small wooden sign marking the split in the trail. Within twenty minutes, they came to the cove that Max had carefully described to her in great detail.

Standing together on the shore, Chris and Kyle just looked in amazement at their rotten luck. The boat was there but showed only partially above the water. The rest of it was submerged under a large palm tree that had fallen squarely on it.

"Be sure to remind me to tell Max that his choice of mooring really sucks," Kyle said sarcastically.

"Now what do we do?" Chris asked dismally.

She couldn't think of any way to salvage their plan. Peering up at Kyle, she realized that the rain was finally letting up, and she could just make out his features in the first early tinges of daylight. In that moment, she knew that simply hiding out in the jungle wasn't an option. Her eyes narrowing, she was happy to see the same resolve in Kyles gaze. "I think it's time we went on the offensive."

Thirty-two

Chris
Tuesday, 4:30 A.M.

"What are you thinking?"

Chris chose her words carefully, knowing how resistant he'd been before to doing anything he considered too risky. "Draw them out. Reduce their numbers. I'm willing to bet that when the odds are evened up, whoever is left will abandon the hostages in favor of saving their own asses."

There was a long, pregnant pause as Kyle studied Chris's face, obviously weighing what she said. Wiping away some mud from his forehead, he finally grimaced and reluctantly shook his head. "That's a tempting scenario, Chris, but considering everything, not the smartest."

Her face started to burn with resentment at what could be considered a condescending comment, but Chris checked herself. He was right. As much as she wanted to seek revenge and help Kyle accomplish his goals against

Jose … she was leading with her emotions, not her head. Looking down at her feet, she fought back the natural instinct to fight and instead forced a rational observation.

"So, I wait it out," she mumbled, shifting the weight of her backpack from one shoulder to the other. "You go through with the exchange. Chang gets away."

"I'll send help for you after we get back to the mainland. Someone should be out here by tomorrow at the latest." Lifting Chris's chin, Kyle looked at her intently with more emotion in his features than she'd seen since she'd met him. "I don't care anymore about my assignment, Chris. I'll gladly walk away from it once I see Jose and the others captured. I have contacts within the Guatemalan government that will be thrilled to move in on his camp. He'll pay for what he's done here."

Finding it hard to speak while caught in his gaze, Chris cleared her throat and took a small step back when he dropped his hand from her face. "What if things go wrong, and you aren't able to make that call?" she asked. It was a legitimate concern. "George isn't going to survive until the ferry comes three days from now."

"You know if you asked him, George wouldn't want us to put the lives of the others at risk for him."

Getting angry again, Chris started to pace in the wet, knee-high grass surrounding them. "Right. But how can you be so sure Jose isn't going to decide they're *all* too much of a liability?"

"If he were going to kill them, it would have happened on the first night," Kyle argued. "Jose is a lot of things, but he likes to believe he does things for some sort of misdirected, noble calling. If he thought killing them was necessary to accomplish what he sees as his destiny, he'd have no qualms about it. Otherwise, it would be a disrespectful act and something below his status. I know," he insisted when he saw the expression Chris gave him, "it's twisted, but that's the truth of it. So long as we don't give him a reason, they're safe. Which is why *you* need to stay hidden out here. I'll tell them you drowned in that river back there. That's even more believable than my shooting you."

Unsatisfied, Chris stopped her pacing and adjusted the gun under her sweatshirt. With everything soaking wet, she was likely to have blisters from the leather chaffing. "If only there was a way to get to a radio or something!" she shouted in frustration. The backpack slipped from her shoulder, and she caught the strap at the last moment, saving the electronics still packed inside from hitting the ground.

Staring down at the bag, she froze. The laptop. "Oh my God," she exclaimed, jerking her head up to look at Kyle. "My laptop."

His face clouding with confusion, Kyle spread his hands wide. "Yeah. Your laptop. What about it?"

"What kind of system do you think that PC uses back at the house?"

Kyle's eyes widened slightly in comprehension. "You think there's some way to tie it into the SAT uplink on the PC? But the whole thing burned up, Chris."

"We have an IT specialist sitting back at that house! And I'm willing to bet there's some sort of *external* application involved to the SAT system that wasn't damaged. If it's possible, I'm sure Ken could figure it out."

Nodding now, Kyle broke out in a grin. "Maybe. You might be right. If you can manage to get it working within an hour after we leave, that would give the Coast Guard time to intervene."

Grabbing Chris's hand as the rain started to pick up again, Kyle led her out of the clearing and into a reasonably protected grove of trees. "It's about 4:30 now. I'll leave by five so that I get back before anyone else comes looking for me, but late enough that we'll be getting ready to leave. Wait for half an hour after I'm gone, and then make your way back to your cabin. Hide out near there and when you see us leaving on the boat, get your ass back to the house and see what Ken can do."

Rain dripped from the foliage overhead, but most of the wind was kept out of the small stand of trees as Chris sat back on her heels and strained to make out Kyle's shape among the shadows. The idea of cowering in the jungle while he went off to an unknown fate still didn't sit well with her. "I know there are times when you have to admit failure, Kyle, but I've never been very good at it. Even though I know you're right, if you weren't here to point out the obvious to me, I'd probably have already gone charging in there and made a bad situation worse. I admire your confidence," she said, searching for him again in the dark. It was easier to admit her own shortcomings when she couldn't see his face. "I'm always questioning my own perception and I'm defensive as a result of it."

"There's nothing wrong with your judgement, Chris," he reassured her. Kneeling down next to her, he reached out somewhat hesitantly to brush the damp hair back from her cheek.

She fought the urge to pull away, feeling suddenly vulnerable; but he left his hand in her hair, and it had a calming effect.

"You're just passionate about what you feel," he continued. "It might get you into trouble sometimes, but it's also what puts you in a class above the rest. Anyone would be lucky to have you as a partner."

Kyle's assessment was something she'd needed to hear for a long time. Coming from him, she believed it, and she felt the last of her reservations fall away. His hand traveled to her cheek and she turned into it, longing for his touch. It was easy … almost *too* easy to let the world reduce itself to this single moment in time. All that mattered anymore was the longing, the need for her to be consumed by him.

Then his arms were around her, and she rose up to meet him in a passionate embrace. His lips found hers in the twilight, and she reached out to pull him in closer, until their bodies were indistinguishable from each other.

Gasping at the electric pulses coursing through her body, Kyle responded by laying her down on the jungle floor. Pulling at her clothes, the break in contact made her body ache, and when they came back together, the breath caught in her throat in a silent moan. New sensations were revealed to her, an awakening of needs that she never knew she had. They reminded her of the raw power of the storm still raging around them.

Pausing, Kyle forced them to slow down, and he pulled back just enough so they could look at each other. In the faint light of the new day, his intense eyes found hers. This time, she fell willingly into them, at once lost, but found at the same time.

Thirty-three

Kyle
Tuesday, 6:30 A.M.

It was hard to focus.

Doing his best to keep his thoughts on task, Kyle absently observed how the swollen stream had already dropped dramatically. The rocks that they'd barely managed to balance on only two hours before were now only partially submerged.

Scrambling up the muddy slope, he followed the trail that was easily found in the daylight, especially since their footprints were still visible. He caught himself comparing his larger boot print to Chris's, and shook his head.

Now's not the time to get soft, he chastised himself. But the memory of the way she felt under him was still too vivid.

Stopping for a moment, Kyle rubbed roughly at his face and took a deep breath. The air was incredibly humid, laden with the recent torrential rain. Not feeling any better, he forced himself to start walking again.

It had been years since he'd felt this way about anyone, and it was incredibly tempting to be caught up in the stimulating emotions. Chris reached a part of him he feared was long gone. But it was a dangerous game to play when so much was at stake. One misstep and there'd be no going back. He couldn't afford to be distracted.

Stepping out onto the beach, he gazed out at the angry ocean and froze. His mind was instantly cleared of any romantic thoughts at the sight of a boat tied up at the main dock.

It was early.

Picking up his pace, Kyle rushed towards the main house. Could Jose have already sent someone out to look for him? It was entirely possible that Carlos was out there now, on a different trail. All he'd have to do is stumble across the clear signs they left behind, and it would lead him right to Chris.

But as he leapt up the steps of the porch, he was relieved to hear Carlos speaking loudly with Jose. He wasn't as concerned about Felipe and Fredrick. Chris could likely handle them.

Yanking the door open, the conversation promptly cut off. Kyle took in the scene and appropriately adjusted his expression and mannerism.

"It's about time," Carlos barked.

Kyle caught a quick glance between the two men and looked beyond them. Felipe was poised at the entrance to the rec room, his attention split between the hostages and them. Fredrick was standing at the open door of the radio room, his back to them as he spoke to someone he couldn't see, likely Ricky. The squawk of a radio buzzed under their voices.

"The boat's early," Kyle grumbled. The tension was palpable and put him further on edge. He did his best to downplay it. "The damn jungle is a mess. Going out there was a waste of time."

Karen appeared near Felipe, looking concerned. "Did you find Chris?" she asked. "Is she okay?"

Jose was staring at Kyle. The intensity of his gaze was unwavering, and he didn't even turn at Karen's interruption. "Well?" was all he said.

"She's dead," Kyle announced bluntly. "I followed her tracks to where the trail slid into a flooded stream. Took me a couple of hours to find her body, but she drowned."

Karen was already crying before he'd finished, and her wailing brought both Dorothy and Max to her side. Kyle idly wondered if Rico's concussion was more serious than they thought, because he would expect him to be the first one there to comfort her. He fought down a twinge of guilt. She'd get over it soon enough.

"It's my fault," Karen insisted, turning into Dorothy's embrace. "I took her hiking out there Saturday and showed her those trails. She probably thought she'd be safe in the meadow."

"Get back in the room!" Jose ordered before Dorothy or anyone else could even try to console her. He left no room for argument, and Max ushered the women back out of view, after throwing a venomous look at Kyle.

"What's with the shortwave?" Kyle asked when the silence dragged out and Jose had simply continued to stare. Did he believe Chris was dead? The man was impossible to read.

"Ricky sent it," Jose replied evenly. "They're getting it set up now. It's more reliable than the one on the boat."

"But I thought we were shoving off an hour before we contact Chang," Kyle said, looking back and forth between Carlos and Jose. "We'll be late to the drop if we wait."

"Plans change," Carlos snarled, squaring off with Kyle.

Turning to face the challenge in the other man's voice, Kyle saw movement at the door to the radio room. Pausing, he shifted his attention in time to see Ricky emerge, holding some random wires and wearing what can only be described as a shit-eating grin on his face. Only, his name wasn't really Ricky, it was Steven Williams.

Already uneasy and in motion, Kyle was reaching for his gun before he was aware of the thought even forming. But he was too late.

As he turned towards Jose with his weapon in hand, the room exploded with a gunshot. Stunned, Kyle watched his weapon fly from his suddenly numb arm an instant before both the percussion and pain hit him.

Thirty-four

Kyle
Tuesday, 7:00 A.M.

Stumbling backwards from the impact, pain blossomed across Kyle's chest. He fell against the closed front door and slid down the wall, his legs unable to hold him up. His left hand went automatically to the wound on the right side of his chest in a vain attempt to stop the flow of blood.

Looking up at Jose as he stepped towards him, he wasn't surprised to see the gun in his hand. He'd underestimated him. Expecting a final bullet in his head, Kyle almost welcomed the release.

"You've betrayed me." It wasn't a question or even an accusation, but more of a profound statement. "Of all my men, Kyle, I thought I could trust you."

"Just kill me and get it over with," Kyle spat, unwilling to play his games any longer. "I don't have to justify myself to you, you freaking nut. I won't be the one to slip the cuffs on, but you've got to know that it *will* happen." Laughing now, Kyle took pleasure in the dark fury on Jose's face. "I've turned over enough information on you to shut your *whole* organization down. They know who you are, where you are, and most importantly, *what* you are. The only reason you aren't already sitting in a cell is because you aren't important enough, you sad sack of shit."

"Enough!" Carlos bellowed, kicking Kyle in the chest hard enough to crack some ribs.

"No!" Jose ordered, putting a hand out towards Carlos.

Doubled over against the door, Kyle was prepared for a further beating and was confused when it stopped. His lungs burning, he winced at the effort to take a breath and looked warily at Jose. The other man was eerily calm. He'd even holstered his pistol. Waving over his shoulder, he motioned for Steven to come forward.

"Tell me," Jose said casually, squatting down a few feet from Kyle so he could look him evenly in the eyes. "Your friend here worked with you, what, six years ago?" he asked, turning back to glance momentarily at the other man.

"About that," Steven confirmed.

Steven was as American as they came, with blonde hair, blue eyes, and a jaw like Rock Hudson. He was part of the first big drug sting Kyle was involved in as a junior agent. He spent hours with the man in the back of a van on a stakeout, and they were both on the interrogation team. Steven worked for the local law enforcement agency in New Mexico. It was a collaborative deployment. What in the *hell* was he doing in South America?

He'd known all along that it was only a matter of time before some of his circles intermingled and he'd run the risk of being recognized, but now? Kyle didn't believe in coincidences.

Looking beyond Jose, he had a hard time focusing on the other man. He was losing too much blood. Frustrated at his inability to make sense of the situation, he squeezed his eyes briefly and shook his head in an attempt to clear it.

"I know, Amigo," Jose taunted, patting Kyle on the leg. "It's confusing. Fortunately, Carlos isn't as trusting as I am. He's been doing some digging. And when our mutual friend here approached him recently, offering some information in exchange for a very reasonable sum … he took it upon himself to arrange a meeting. It was supposed to occur before our departure, but Steven missed the boat, so to say."

Chuckling at his bad joke, Jose stood back up and wiped his hands slowly on his pants, as if touching Kyle had soiled them. "Steven located Ricky yesterday. After confirming some radio chatter that indicated there was a search underway for a missing American *agent*, they decided it best if Steven delivered his message to me in person. And you know what, Kyle? It was well worth the cost. I believe the storm was divine intervention," he continued, switching topics. Smiling, he tilted his head as he studied Kyle. "You see, it will all work out. Only, not for you."

His grin fading, he turned towards Fredrick. The hostages were huddled behind him, watching the scene unfold.

"You! Come here. Stop the bleeding."

Karen cringed at the demand, but Jose was clearly pointing at her and she didn't dare disagree. Rushing forward, she went to Kyle and kneeled down next to him. Pulling his blood-soaked t-shirt up, she exposed a raw, ragged hole. It was high and off to the side, almost in his armpit. The bullet appeared to have gone through, leaving an even larger exit wound just below his right shoulder blade.

Kyle looked down and made the vague observation that at least it wasn't a sucking chest wound, so his lung wasn't likely punctured. Honestly, it was harder to breathe on the left side where Carlos had kicked him.

Jose dropped a towel in his lap, and Kyle regarded the other man apprehensively. It was a bad sign that he wanted him alive.

As Karen picked the cloth up and pressed it against his chest, he did his best not to react to the incredible amount of pain it induced. Shifting his weight, Kyle was able to reach across himself and hold the direct pressure with his left hand. Smiling at Karen, he nodded his thanks.

"Go get the woman," Jose said abruptly. He was speaking to Carlos but was still staring at Kyle. "She's not dead. Bring her back."

Kyle did his best not to give Jose the gratification of seeing his distress. He knew the man was twisted, but he didn't think he'd jeopardize his exchange with Chang to seek revenge. He had to have something specific in mind.

"Damnit, Jose, am I supposed to wave a magic wand and make her walk out of the jungle? She could hide from us for days."

Shooting an icy glare at Carlos, Jose lunged forward and grabbed Karen brutally by the back of the neck. Yanking the small woman to her feet, he shoved her at him. Stumbling over Kyle's prone body, she cried out in shock as she fell into Carlos, who easily caught her.

"She'll be close by," Jose barked. "And I'm guessing she'll be tempted to help her friend. Use your imagination."

Sneering, Carlos took hold of Karen's arm and marched her back across the room. Kyle was thankful to see Max silently keeping the other guests at bay. An attempt at intervention by any of them at this point would mean instant death.

As Kyle tried to get to his feet, Carlos shoved him out of the way so he could open the front door. Feeling powerless to stop him, he put his good hand out to catch himself and was rewarded with a stream of fresh blood down his side. Cursing, Kyle sat back down, hard, and watched helplessly through the open door as Carlos and Karen disappeared from view.

Thirty-five

Chris
Tuesday, 7:00 A.M.

Something was wrong.

Chris had been watching the boat for about ten minutes. Hidden in the thick foliage near her cabin, she hated the vulnerability she was experiencing. It had to be close to seven by now. They should at least be *preparing* to leave. Squinting against the rising sun, she studied the length of the dock to where it disappeared from view. Although it was a ways off in the distance, she should still be able to see if anyone was on it.

Something was wrong.

Chris's head snapped up at the sound of a gunshot, the echo bouncing off the jungle to her back. She couldn't be sure, but it sounded like a smaller caliber than the .45 Kyle carried.

Straining to listen, she sighed in relief when the silence stretched out. If they were executing the hostages, there would have been a quick succession of shots.

Suppressing a shudder at the scene her thoughts produced, Chris instead focused on the other possibilities.

The boat was there early, but they weren't loading it. Was there an issue with the guy, Ricky? It didn't sound like anyone really knew him. That was probably the best scenario. The most likely one, however, was that Jose didn't believe Kyle's story. She *knew* it was a bad idea.

Looking back up the trail that led to the house, Chris rocked on the balls of her feet, itching to run towards it. As much as she wanted to rush in and do something foolish, that wouldn't help anyone. Her lower lip began to tremble as the realization sunk in that Kyle might be lying somewhere dead. A cold trickle of dread slowly uncoiled in her chest, and her breaths began to come in quick, ragged gasps.

Chris immediately recognized the symptoms of an anxiety attack and teetered briefly on the edge. It would be so easy to just give into the raw fear and escape within herself.

But that wasn't who she was. Swallowing around the knot in her throat, she instead closed her eyes and counted slowly, matching her breathing to the rhythm. After a couple of minutes of forced meditation, her heart rate leveled out and she began to think clearly again.

She was standing next to a palm tree, holding onto the rough surface like a boat's mast in a storm. Raising her forehead from where it had been resting against the trunk, she took a slow, measured step back. The birds were starting to return to the trees, and the exotic music had an additional calming effect.

Realizing she was leaving herself exposed so close to the trail, Chris crouched down among the fragrant ferns and moss. Her eyes wide, she had unconsciously switched from being the hunted to the hunter. While she wasn't going to rush into anything, neither was she going to run away into the trees. Slipping off the backpack in order to leave herself more mobile, she adjusted the holster under her sweatshirt and prepared to circle around the property and approach the main house from the back gardens.

But before she even took her first step, a familiar voice called out to her.

"Chri-is!"

The singsong tone made Carlos sound even more threatening. Instantly chilled by the implications, Chris shifted her focus back towards the beach where the sound was coming from.

"Your friend, Karen, would like to speak with you, Chris!"

Slipping silently up to the back corner of her cabin as he continued calling her name, Chris could clearly see the couple making their way up the beach. Carlos had ahold of Karen by her hair. A huge fist of it was balled up in his meaty hand. Her expression was a mixture of pain and horror as he also pressed a gun into the side of her head.

They were moving somewhat awkwardly in the deep sand. It was rapidly drying out under the hot sun that was breaking through the last of the clouds being blown away. The rain was gone, but the sea behind them still held onto the final remnants of the hurricane, tossing whitecaps and spray high into the air.

Karen was much shorter than Carlos was, but he was holding her close so that it would be very difficult to shoot him without also striking her. Even so, Chris's first instinct was to draw her Kymber and line him up in her laser sights. Huffing in defeat, she lowered it just as fast. Maybe if she were ten feet away she'd take the shot, but never from that distance.

"I'm going to keep this simple," Carlos bellowed, stopping right in front of the cabin. "Jose doesn't think you're dead and, frankly, I don't care either way. If you aren't, then it's likely you're hanging out nearby. So listen up. I'm giving you one opportunity to save your friends life. Because I also don't give a shit if *she* lives or dies."

Karen began to openly cry, finally breaking down. It only encouraged Carlos, and he pulled her even closer to him, leaning down so his face was next to hers.

"I'll give ya a couple of minutes. And then I'm putting a bullet in her pretty head."

Chris believed him.

"Chris … *Please*," Karen begged in between her sobs.

Carlos drew the hammer back on the gun.

Karen closed her eyes and began praying in Spanish.

Chris jammed the pistol into the front pocket of her sweatshirt and, without hesitation, stepped out from the cover of the undergrowth. Holding her hands out in a submissive gesture, she walked towards them until she was less than ten feet away. Her mind raced, calculating her options. While she would gladly give her own life for that of her young, pregnant friend, she had no delusions of what was going to happen.

She had to assume that Kyle was dead. While her compliance at the moment might prevent immediate death for Karen, if they were successfully returned to the house, Chris figured that ultimately the outcome would be the same.

Breaking into a wide grin, Carlos almost seemed surprised at his success. Motioning with the gun for her to come closer, he shoved Karen to the ground with the intent of pulling Chris into her place.

It was the opening she needed.

In a surprise move, she lunged forward as he stepped towards her, bringing them together much faster than he expected. In the same motion, Chris reached out for the forearm of his gun hand, latching on and twisting so that her back was to him. Using the momentum, she forced his arm down with all her strength, raising her right knee up at the same time, and effectively knocking the weapon from his grasp.

It all happened so fast that Carlos barely had a chance to react, but as soon as he began to resist, any advantage Chris had was gone. While they were around the same height, the man had a good eighty pounds on her. She felt the muscles in his arm and chest flex just before her knee struck his fist, and she was caught up in a vice-like bear hug before she could push away.

Her back still to him, she managed to reach into her sweatshirt pocket as he literally lifted her off the ground. Growling obscenities in her ear, Carlos carried her several steps to the right before body slamming her on the harder surface of the wet sand.

Chris's head bounced off the ground, and her vision dimmed slightly before a wave splashed over her. Gagging and coughing on the briny saltwater that filled her mouth, she still had enough sense about her to try to pull the gun out. Fumbling with it as the sights caught on her wet sweatshirt, Carlos dragged her to her feet, oblivious of the weapon.

Grabbing her roughly by the hair and yanking her head back, he forced her to look into his dark, cold eyes that reminded Chris of a snake. "I think it's time a real man taught you a lesson," he snarled, pulling her up against him.

"I don't think so," Chris whispered, just before she pulled the trigger.

Thirty-six

Kyle
Tuesday 7:15 A.M.

"Is it ready?" Jose was talking to Steven, and the new man on the scene was definitely weary of the Guerrilla leader.

"Umm ... just about sir," he answered, sticking his head out through the door of the radio room. "I needed to tie the SAT phone into the existing shortwave antennae, because there's still a lot of atmospheric disturbance from the storm, but -- "

"Just tell me when I can make the call!"

"Five minutes," Steven assured him, ducking back inside the room.

Kyle could hear him cursing to Felipe as the two of them apparently worked to get their communications back online.

It still wasn't clear why he was alive. He'd managed to get himself into one of the cushioned seats in the front lobby and the direct pressure seemed to be working to stop the flow of blood. Now that the initial shock to his system had passed, it was replaced with a hot, searing pain and a headache. At least the strength returned to his legs and he could think more clearly.

Although his right arm was useless, Kyle still couldn't help but glance at his gun. It was resting against a potted ficus tree, taunting him a good fifteen feet away. Sitting there while his fate was determined by a crazy fanatic wasn't something he'd let happen without a fight, as weak as it might be.

Fredrick threw a fresh hand towel at him before going to stand on the other side of the seating area. Staring at him, his contempt was palpable, and Kyle didn't even try to talk with him as he swapped out the makeshift bandages.

"What agency are you with?" Jose asked without preamble.

"C.I.A."

The other man seemed mildly surprised at Kyle's forthrightness. "You have been with them for ten years," he replied.

Kyle sighed heavily. "Aren't we past this stage?" he asked, leaning forward slightly and wincing at the pain the movement rewarded him with. "You already know everything about me, Jose. If Benedict Arnold in there is anything more than an amateur, he will have sold you a full dossier on me. So let's cut through the bull and get to the point. What do you want?"

"Here," Steven walked rapidly up to Jose, holding the SAT phone out. "We got him."

Grabbing the device, Jose ignored Kyle's question

and launched into an animated conversation that was broken up by static and random clicks and squelches. In spite of the interference, he successfully convinced the reclusive dealer to change the location and time of their meeting. But it wasn't without something to sweeten the deal.

Kyle listened intently to the one side of the conversation.

"Yes, you heard correctly, Mr. Chang. A CIA operative … How I acquired him is not important, but I have heard that you have a … shall we say, market, for someone with his credentials?" Nodding happily, Jose looked up at Kyle to make sure he caught the next part. "I also have a personal gift for you. I understand you've got a special taste for American women?" Laughing now, he watched the expression on Kyle's face with obvious pleasure.

So, revenge it was. Leaning forward in an attempt to stand up, Kyle found himself forcefully shoved back into the seat by Fredrick. "You won't get away with this!" he said feebly, angry at himself for his weakness.

Disconnecting the call, Jose leveled him with a stony gaze. "I already have."

Tossing the blockish phone back at Steven, Jose turned to address Felipe, who had taken up the position at the rec room. The hostages were ordered to retreat deeper into the room when Carlos left, and the silence from inside was heavy.

"You and Steven get the boat loaded. We leave in an hour. And, Felipe," he added, lowering his voice. "Bring me the extra ammo Steven brought. We'll need to tie up a few loose ends before we go." Scowling at Kyle, he narrowed his eyes and spoke slowly. "We'll wait for Chris to join us. I want to make sure she remembers what she brought upon her friends."

Chilled by the statement, Kyle thought of the young boy and other captives. He'd failed them all.

Thirty-seven

Chris
Tuesday, 7:30 A.M.

"That's good enough."

Chris stood back and checked out their handiwork. It was a grueling task, but with each woman taking an arm, she and Karen had managed to drag Carlos off the beach and out of sight of the boat.

The shot was muffled enough between their bodies that she didn't think the sound carried far enough to be heard at the main house. She was counting on it. The element of surprise was the only thing she had going for her.

Looking down at the corpse, she considered herself lucky. She'd nestled the gun up under his ribcage, and the bullet must have gone right through his heart. Carlos was dead by the time he hit the sand.

"What do we do now?" Karen asked, her eyes still wide with shock.

Chris worried about her. This kind of stress could

force a miscarriage. Walking briskly out into the open to retrieve Carlos' dropped gun, she then returned to the shadows behind the cabin.

"*We* aren't doing anything," she said forcefully. Taking Karen's hand, she placed the pistol in it. "*You* are going to hide in the cabin. If any of those terrorist open the door, you shoot them."

"Who are you?"

Chris stared intently at Karen, weighing her answer. "I'm a cop," she said simply. "A detective with the Seattle police department. I didn't say anything before because I really just wanted to have a relaxing vacation."

A long moment of silence dragged out between the two women, until Karen started to laugh, a sound dangerously close to being hysterical. Unable to resist, Chris joined her and the two of them laughed at the absolute absurdity of the situation until tears were streaming down their faces. Pulling the other woman into a tight embrace, Chris whispered into her ear.

"I promise you, I'm going to do everything I can to stop them."

***

David had a very bad feeling. Well, okay … the past two days were pretty much one big, bad feeling. But the atmosphere had shifted when that new guy arrived. After Kyle was shot, which was confusing as hell, he got the distinct sense that they were being ignored. He would normally consider that a *good* thing, but under the present circumstances, it felt ... dismissive. Like, it didn't matter anymore if they were talking to each other, or had water or anything.

He was trying to hear what was being said in the other room. Ignoring his dad's silent protest, he moved as close to the entrance as he dared. Jose was barking orders, including to bring back some extra bullets, and then he lowered his voice so that David couldn't make the rest out.

Yeah, a *really* bad feeling.

When Fredrick briefly stepped out of sight, David made an impulsive decision. Dashing across the open space, he nearly fell head first into the shadowy den. Almost in a panic, he aimed for the only source of light: a small window on the far wall.

He'd been daydreaming about this escape plan for nearly thirty-six hours. He noticed it the one time he used the room, but since that first night, there was always an armed guard stationed outside the door. He didn't even know if it was shuttered like the front windows, or if he would be able to squeeze through it. It was likely that no one else had even thought of it as a possible means of exit for those reasons. But he was small for his age. He was also skinny. And desperate.

Throwing the latch, he cringed at the slight creaking noise the old panes of glass made as he swung them on their hinges. They opened like French doors, and thankfully, there was nothing but an overgrown bush on the other side. Stealing a quick, nervous glance over his shoulder, David fully expected to see Felipe or Fredrick barreling down on him. Surprised to find the room still empty, he lifted himself up and went through the small opening head first.

Man, his dad was going to be *pissed*. Or maybe not. Because if Jose was going to kill them, then his dad would *want* him to escape. A twinge of guilt coursed through David as he wiggled and struggled to get his butt through. He'd fantasized some grand schemes of rescue, but now that the moment was here, he had no idea what the hell he was going to do once he was free.

Teetering on the windowsill, the edge cut painfully into his hipbones. The sensation that his feet would be grabbed was enough to make him hyperventilate, and he made ragged wheezing sounds through his clenched teeth.

Finally, gravity won, and he put his arms up to protect his face as he fell into the bush. Suffering a few minor scrapes on the way down, he rolled twice before coming to a stop in the damp grass of the side garden.

A startled gasp caused him to freeze mid-crouch, and he looked up into the barrel of a very intimidating gun. A little urine leaked out before he realized that it was Chris holding it.

***

"David!" Chris whispered, startled to see the teen.

When he remained frozen even after she lowered the gun, she leaned forward and grabbed him by his shirt. "Come on." Not waiting for an answer, or compliance, she literally half dragged him around the back corner of the house.

"Okay! I'm okay!" Tugging at his shirt, David pulled it from Chris's hand and did his best to compose himself, hoping that the damp grass covered up any spots on his shorts.

Shushing him, Chris continued their march until they were well hidden in the back gardens. Turning to the young man, she marveled at his tenacity. "Good job, David."

Blushing, he struggled to compose himself. "No biggie. I just waited for them get distracted."

"What's happening? I heard a shot and Carlos came looking for me. Karen's okay," she added, cutting of his question. "Carlos isn't."

Grinning at the blunt report, he tried his best to mimic the older woman's coolness. "This new dude showed up with the boat, and there was this, like, really tense meeting with all of them. Then, when that Kyle guy came back, Jose shot him." David felt a little envious at the extreme emotion that little tidbit created on Chris's face, but he was quick to set her straight. "He's fine. I mean, he's shot in the chest, I think, but he's still talkin' and stuff."

Chris closed her eyes at the news that Kyle was still

alive. Karen had tried to reassure her that the wound wasn't life threatening, but she had half-convinced herself the other woman was only trying to placate her. Her emotions threatened to take over, and so instead of giving in to the relief, Chris harnessed it to use for motivation. "Where is he at?"

"Who, Kyle? He's in the front registration area. So is Jose. But he just told Fredrick and the new guy to go get the boat ready, so that'll just leave him and Felipe. One of them will have to watch ... um, us. I guess they might notice I'm gone. But they aren't paying much attention to us, Chris. I think maybe they're going to kill everyone."

His voice caught on the last sentence, betraying his fear, and Chris reached out to take his hand. "Stay hidden. I'm going to try and make my way out towards the boat before those guys get there."

Leaving him before he had a chance to argue with her, Chris sprinted back the way she came. It was the best opportunity she was going to have for an ambush.

Flying through the jungle as fast as she dared, she cut back over to the southern cabin trail and then out onto the beach. Running through the sand, she turned north, back towards the house, but kept to the tree line. It would eventually end at the other trailhead that ran east, from the dock to the main house. Her only hope was that she was faster than the men were and that they were still on that trail. She didn't have to necessarily kill them, just make sure they weren't mobile.

Hunkering down behind the same sign she noted on the first day of her vacation, Chris didn't have to wait long. The loud conversation announced the men's arrival long before she saw them, so she had her gun drawn and sights lined up by the time their heads bobbed into view.

Thirty-eight

Kyle
Tuesday, 7:45 A.M.

The two shots were thunderous.

Jose leapt to his feet and looked at Felipe, startled. The other man flew out of his chair in the entrance of the rec room and stood looking around, wild-eyed.

Kyle had no doubt it was Chris's Kymber. Jose, of course, had no reason to suspect such a thing. "I told Carlos I wanted her *alive*," he spat. Hesitating, he considered his options. "If she is dead, Chang will have to settle for the comatose woman," he decided. "I said nothing about her state of mind."

Felipe nodded his agreement and turned to reposition his chair. As he glanced into the room, he automatically took a headcount. Hesitating, he counted again.

"What are you doing?"

Turning back to Jose, Felipe's expression said it all.

His face flushing a deep red, Jose stormed into the

recreation room and turned the lights up. Taking in the familiar scene, he passed over the unconscious form of George. Rico was sprawled on the other couch, still in the throes of an intense headache and nearly oblivious of anything else.

The blonde woman was still perched on the loveseat near the burned out fire with Dorothy and Esmerelda huddled on either side. Turning his scowl on Max and Ken, seated at the chess table, he took a threatening step towards them.

"Where's the boy?" he demanded, sweeping the pieces onto the floor. Taking his gun out, he pointed it towards Dorothy.

"He went out the window in the den!" Max yelled. "He's just a child," he continued earnestly. "Why does it even matter?"

"On your feet!" Jose shoved Max when he didn't respond fast enough. "All of you. In front of the fireplace!"

Kyle could hear the exchange from the other room. Waiting patiently, he was finally rewarded with the opening he knew would eventually present itself.

Felipe turned his back on him.

Unsure if his legs would hold him, he ignored the new levels of pain exploding through his chest as he pushed himself to his feet. Lurching forwards, he made it four steps before two things happened. Felipe either saw or sensed the movement, and Kyle's legs collapsed. Fortunately, the later happened a fraction sooner, so the bullet meant for his head lodged itself in the mahogany beam behind him.

Falling into the ficus tree, Kyle reached blindly for the gun he knew was somewhere under him. As his hand closed around the cold steel, an odd howling sound filled the room, and he looked up in time to see David plow into Felipe, causing the next shot to also go wide.

Rolling over onto his elbows, Kyle steadied his weapon and took a shot just as Felipe threw the boy from his back and stood up. Falling in an unceremonious heap, Felipe began to groan loudly and distracted Kyle for a fraction of a second too long.

"Ah!" David shrieked, but it was the sound of fear, not victory.

Pivoting, Kyle discovered that Jose had the boy by the neck and was slowly backing towards the sunroom at the rear of the house.

"Let him go, Jose. It's over. This is only going to make it worse."

"You are delusional, my friend," Jose countered. "I have a boat, I have the money, and you will never find me!"

"You're wrong about that."

Jose stumbled at the sound of Chris's voice coming from behind him. Turning just far enough so he could keep both the front and back door in sight, he saw that she was standing in the opening to the gardens.

"I'm afraid you're on your own." Dumping one of the heavy duffle bags at her feet, she kicked it for emphasis. "Your guy dropped this."

As the significance of the presence of the money

sank in, Jose's nostrils flared and the whites of his eyes flashed.

Chris raised her weapon slowly and deliberately. The playful light in her eyes disappeared, and the full force of her intense gaze enveloped Jose. They were less than ten feet apart.

Maybe it was the twitch of Jose's arm, or another nuance Kyle couldn't see, but as the percussion of her weapon filled the room, he only had one thought.

They were free.

Thirty-nine

Chris
Tuesday, 8:00 P.M.

Digging her bare feet into the hot sand, Chris silently watched what was perhaps the most magnificent sunset of her life. She figured that the remnants of the hurricane lent to the effect and was responsible for what looked like fiery mountains exploding along the horizon.

Closing her eyes, she let the offshore breeze lift and playfully blow her hair around. A part of her wondered if it could erase any of the stain that the past three days left behind. Pulling her knees to her chest under her sundress, she lowered her forehead to rest against them and hugged them tight.

No. Nothing would ever make this okay.

Chris sensed, more than heard, Kyle lower himself onto the sand beside her. They had wanted to evacuate him with George on the first boat out, but he'd refused. Knowing he wouldn't touch her without an invite, she took the first step and leaned into his good side, welcoming the arm that went around her.

"They're finally done with all of the interviews, but forensics will be here until tomorrow. We just got confirmation that Chang's boat was successfully intercepted." He paused, letting the meaning of that statement sink in. "We'll be leaving with the Coast Guard in about an hour."

Nodding, Chris finally looked up. It was almost dark. The intense running lights on the boats at the dock were beginning to cut across the water, highlighting the waves. Turning to Kyle, she studied his features for a minute before reaching out to pull his face down to hers for a brief, gentle kiss.

"I'm glad you're okay." Kyle grinned at her in response, and she was surprised to notice he had a dimple in his left cheek. She briefly traced it with a finger before letting her hand fall back to her knee.

"All the hostages are okay, thanks to you."

Chris shook her head at the compliment. "Let's not forget our young hero."

Laughing, Kyle pulled her against him a little tighter. "Yeah. His version gets a little better with each telling.

"Jose and Carlos are the only deaths … besides Desmond," he added. "George is already in surgery on the mainland, and the prognosis going in was good." When Chris only answered with a small nod, he studied her silhouette. "You know you did the right thing."

"Did I?"

"You did exactly what every active shooter and hostage training scenario told you to do: you took the shot. And David's alive because of it."

Chris was silent for several minutes. "Is that why I did it?" The question was a whisper.

"You're the only one who can answer that," Kyle replied after a brief hesitation. "I may not know you very well, Chris, but the experience we just went through tends to expose some truths. Regardless of what you think of yourself, I saw someone that was incredibly brave and unselfish. I *know* I've got some work to do when I get back home, but you helped me take the first steps; and I wanted to thank you while I had a chance."

Both surprised and touched by his insight, Chris leaned in for a deeper kiss. As they separated, she wondered if she would ever see him again once they left the island. She hoped so.

"You know," Kyle began with some hesitation. "We're going to be required to stick around for a while. At least until they're done with the investigation out here, and I imagine the local authorities will want to talk with us."

Hoping he was having the same thoughts, Chris leaned back towards him and let her lips linger just beyond his reach. "What are you suggesting?" Her voice was low and inviting. At least, she hoped it was.

His eyes focused on her mouth, and he let the tension draw out for another beat before pulling her in for a more demanding kiss. Finally breaking apart, he grinned crookedly at her. "I was thinking that after they patch me up, we might be able to spend some time getting to know each other properly."

"That would be nice," Chris whispered, afraid to break the spell she felt they were both under. "So long as we can agree that no weapons will be involved."

"Agreed," Kyle laughed. Standing with some effort, he brushed the sand from his pants and offered her his good hand.

"I'm going to stay just a little longer," she explained, giving his hand a parting squeeze. "I'll get the rest of my things from the cabin before I head back."

With a small wave, Kyle turned away; and she sat watching the empty beach long after he was gone.

Turning back to the warm caress of the sultry breeze, tears finally spilled silently onto her cheeks, fanned into her hair by the wind.

It's okay to cry, she thought with relief. It made her feel … alive.

THE END

ABOUT THE AUTHOR

Tara Meyers resides in the beautiful state of Washington. When she isn't writing, she's out hiking in the rugged Cascade Mountains, or enjoying life with her two amazing kids and several dogs! If you were entertained by this story, you might also like the novels she's written under the pen name of Tara Ellis.

Made in the USA
Middletown, DE
14 January 2020